TIFFANY ACHING'S
GUIDE TO BEING A
WITCH

About the Author

Tiffany Aching hails from the Chalk. Descended from a long line of farmers and shepherds, she began training as a witch at eleven years old after being scouted at age nine by witchfinder, Miss Perspicacia Tick – author of *Fairies and How to Avoid Them*. She has trained under a number of witches, including Mrs Gytha Ogg – author of *The Joye of Snacks* – and was recently named direct successor to Mistress Esmeralda Weatherwax, doyenne of witches.

In less than a decade, Miss Aching has gone from making cheese on her parents' farm, to becoming one of the most respected witches the Disc has ever produced. She has fought off invaders from other realms, led a clan of fearsome pictsies, travelled to lands beyond imagination, communed with gods, expelled evil spirits, and saved countless lives along the way.

She currently lives in a shepherd's hut on the downlands with her cat, You. She still occasionally makes cheese and is currently trying to recreate her grandmother's infamous Special Sheep Liniment recipe. This is her first book.

Hag o' Hags!
– Rob

Dat us, Rob?
– Awfully We
Billy Bigchin

Aye!

Wez in a
bok!?

I is in a bo
Bog off ye
scunner!

TIFFANY ACHING'S
GUIDE TO BEING A
WITCH

With annotations from:

Esmerelda Weatherwax   Nanny Ogg   Miss Tick

And Rob Anybody

Plus helpful corrections from Mrs Letice Earwig

RHIANNA PRATCHETT
& GABRIELLE KENT

ILLUSTRATED BY
PAUL KIDBY

I fink Ive had
0 thems in a kebab!

PENGUIN BOOKS

For Terry Pratchett and Colin Kent, fathers who encouraged their daughters to keep their minds open to magic and wonder, and not to forget to do the hard work. Raising a drop of Special Sheep Liniment in their names.

PENGUIN BOOKS

UK | USA | Canada | Ireland | Australia
India | New Zealand | South Africa

Penguin Books is part of the Penguin Random House group of companies whose addresses can be found at global.penguinrandomhouse.com

www.penguin.co.uk
www.puffin.co.uk
www.ladybird.co.uk

 Penguin Random House UK

 Big Jobs!

First published 2023

003

Text copyright © Dunmanifestin Limited 2023
Illustrations copyright © Paul Kidby 2023

Design by Alex Stott

Printed and bound in Turkey

The authorized representative in the EEA is Penguin Random House Ireland, Morrison Chambers, 32 Nassau Street, Dublin D02 YH68

A CIP catalogue record for this book is available from the British Library

ISBN: 978-0-241-65199-5

All correspondence to:
Penguin Books, Penguin Random House Children's
One Embassy Gardens, 8 Viaduct Gardens, London SW11 7BW

Penguin Random House is committed to a sustainable future for our business, our readers and our planet. This book is made from Forest Stewardship Council® certified paper.

FSC
www.fsc.org

MIX
Paper | Supporting responsible forestry
FSC® C018179

CONTENTS

Esmerelda 'Granny'
Weatherwax

Wotcha, Goatberger!

I'd be grateful if you could slip this in when you print up our Tiff's book. Bit of a surprise for the girl. You can see who's written it, so if you scrimp on Tiff's payment, Esme will be back to haunt you. Death can't stop a Weatherwax!

I'll be in touch soon to talk about *The Joye of Snacks: Vol 2: Nibbles, Wobbles and Extra Banan...* ...

Goatberger... ...

take the ...

gooseberry ...

and the ...

prawns an...

then you giv...

a good sha...

and rub it ...

your chest. ...

pin on the sp...

and just foll...

Wishing ...

Gytha Ogg ...

aka A Lancre ...

Blessings be upon this book.

When you read this I will probably be dead.

No one should feel bad about that. I have lived a life. Feels like several. An' aside from a few questionable buffet selections, I have few regrets.

I can't say as I usually hold with books about witchcraft. But, I have to say that this is the best book that I don't hold with.

Tiffany Aching is a remarkable young woman and a witch to her bones. Heed her words, for the knowledge in these pages has been hard won and not given lightly. She has learned from the best and I believe has surpassed them. She knows what witchcraft is really about when it's stripped to the core. The world needs more witches like her, and hopefully this book will help with that.

I know that in Tiffany Aching, I leave Lancre, the Chalk and beyond in good hands. I wish I were there to see what she'll become, but maybe a part of me will stick around for a while to find out.

Esmerelda Weatherwax

MRS LETICE EARWIG
HIGHER MAGIK, PROFESSIONAL SPELLS

Dear Mr Goatberger,

As the author of many bestselling books on witchcraft, such as *First Flights in Witchcraft*, *The Higher MagiK*, *My Fairy Friends*, and *To Ride a Golden Broomstick*, imagine my surprise when I was not consulted on your most recent acquisition, *Guide to Being a Witch*, by young Tiffany Aching. I have managed to avail myself of a number of pages from this guide and soon discovered an array of omissions and inaccuracies. Please find enclosed my corrections for inclusion. I also enclose my card, should you wish to further avail yourself of my extensive knowledge of magiK, witchcraft and wizardry.

Regards,
Mrs Letice Earwig
(pronounced 'Ah-wij')

Mrs Letice
Earwig

ON BEING A WITCH

Hag!
– Rob

So here you are, holding my book. Perhaps you're already an apprentice witch looking for extra guidance on the future. Maybe you've been earmarked by a witchfinder as someone with 'potential' and you're wondering just what that might mean. Or possibly you're simply curious about what might be in these pages and are looking forward to correcting me, pretending you haven't read it, or treating me with a lethal amount of politeness next time our paths cross. Whether you've bought, begged, borrowed or stolen this book, you are welcome here.

This book was written over a number of years and I've lost some dear friends along the way. Their teachings live on in these pages. As do their notes, which I've retained for posterity. They live on in me. And now, I hope they will live on in you too.

For me, finding my personal path to witch-hood was hazy at
best. But it also involved a book – *The Goode Childe's Booke of
Faerie Tales*. Not exactly a guide to being a witch so much as a
guide to not being one. The teller of these tales clearly imagined
the 'goode childe' would empathize with the noble princes,
beautiful princesses, brave woodcutters and those who abuse the
letter E. Not me. Princes were dull and mostly made of chin. I
didn't have the poise, breeding or the good hair to be a princess.
Besides, they mainly seemed to do daft things with spindles or
apples, or else sat around waiting to be rescued. Their lives were
both dangerous and boring. Woodcutters appeared a little more
competent. But, aside from the occasional break to kill a talking
wolf, I wasn't sure I wanted to chop wood all day. And since I've
never been that good with an axe, we were approaching
dangerous and boring territory again.

Witches, now they seemed *much* more fun. Okay, there was a
certain amount of being shoved in ovens by greedy children or
talking to mirrors, so danger was a given. But witches were
dangerous and *exciting*. They got broomsticks, wands and magic
spells. And, as I imagined back then, they went to learn
witchcraft at a special school. Probably taken there on the back
of a unicorn or something equally magical like that.

But witchcraft isn't about magic or showy spells. At least not
most of the time. It's largely about hard work and realising that
true magic – true *power* – is not about understanding spells, but

understanding people. Hearing their spill words – the things they almost say, but don't or can't. Being a witch is about facing your fears and understanding that even if something isn't your fault, it's your responsibility. It's about being a voice for the voiceless and standing between the light and the darkness. And, more often than not, it's about having a piece of string on you.

If you're still with me, then maybe this is the life for you. I'm glad because the world needs witches and witchcraft. In whatever form they take. As you tread the path you've chosen you will learn the lessons of those who gift you with their wisdom and knowledge. They will become part of you. Because you are not just a witch, you are all witches that have come before you and will come after you. This isn't *really* my book. It is our book. As for the school, it's not a place, it's all places. Just look around you. You're already there.

BECOMING A WITCH

They say that you don't find witchcraft, it finds you. In my case it found me in the form of Miss Perspicacia Tick, a witchfinder. She sensed me with a shamble[1] and, using a saucer of ink as a scrying device, she watched me fend off the water-dwelling monster, Jenny Green-Teeth.

As a witchfinder, Miss Tick searches for potential witches in places where they are unlikely to be otherwise spotted, or where they might suffer hostility from the locals. However, all older witches keep an eye and ear out for young girls who show ability. This doesn't just mean girls who accidentally levitate annoying siblings, or turn bullies into frogs.[2] Okay, *some* witches

1. See Shambles. *Page 72*
2. See Witch Magic. *Page 58*

Although those with such abilities will certainly need identifying so that we can provide some help in controlling them!
– Miss Tick

Waily! Rob

might be discovered by exhibiting such abilities but, as <u>Maeve,</u> the old kelda of the Chalk Hill Feegle clan, told me, it can just be someone who thinks in the right sort of way. Witches typically have first sight – they see what's *really* there rather than what they *assume* should be there, and second thoughts – they observe and think about the way they are thinking. Mentally, they are typically hard, sharp and stubborn. You'll also know a witch by looking for the one running towards trouble rather than away from it.

Hair has a waterweed-like consistency. Useful for hiding in the shallows.
— Miss Tick

Eyes the size of soup plates. 8-inches to be precise. Verified by Miss Aching.

Jenny Green-Teeth

Large clawed hands for grasping and grabbing. Steer clear.

Teeth weaker than they look. Aim here with frying pan or other iron implement.

Reminds me of a lodger we once had. Iron frying pan worked well on him too.
— Nanny Ogg

The Call to Magic

Witchcraft can be learned, but magical ability is often hereditary. Lily, the sister of Mistress Esmerelda Weatherwax was a powerful witch who 'went to the bad'. Her grandmother was a witch who fought vampires and her distant cousin was an Archchancellor of Unseen University, but wizardry doesn't run in families as wizards have strict rules about <u>celibacy</u>. They say it's to prevent their magical powers being drained, but it's actually to prevent the birth of sourcerers.

   Some people are never officially identified as witches. I didn't realize it when she was alive, but my own Granny Aching was a powerful witch who was never discovered by anyone but herself.

Not often I agrees with wizards, but they gets some things right!
- E. Weatherwax

All I can say is, if shaking sheets drains magic then I must have started out as the most powerful witch who ever existed!
— Nanny Ogg

Miss Tick's tent

At least, no one human – she was <u>hag o' the hills</u> to the pictsies. She never called herself a witch, but her very presence on the Chalk was enough to keep the elves of Fairyland from invading our world.

We follow the call to witchcraft for different reasons. Nanny Ogg tells me she started in the craft to get <u>boys</u>, whereas Mistress Weatherwax started out <u>to get even.</u> Me? I did it so that I could look after the hills the way Granny Aching did – so that I could become as good as she was, and return to the Chalk better than I went.

Aye she was a fine hag. Good taste in baccy £. – Rob

Successfully! – Nanny Ogg

More Successfully! –E. Weatherwax

MRS LETICE EARWIG
HIGHER MAGIK, PROFESSIONAL SPELLS

I can categorically state that marital relations have no negative impact whatsoever on magic. In fact, the energy created during the act of passion can be directed towards a specific purpose thus increasing the impact of a spell. The idea that magic is drained by physical relations is actually a fallacy propagated by high-level wizards in order to prevent the birth of sourcerers, which would risk a return to the mage wars. In the Year of the Hyena, there was great magical fallout when a young sourcerer came to power at the Unseen University. There has been much covering up of the magical chaos that ensued in order to prevent non-magical folk from fearing the magically attuned.

Training & Apprenticeships

It's traditional for a young witch to be taken on as an apprentice to an older witch, living with her rent free and paying for training by helping with the chores – in many cases this means doing *all* of the chores! Apprenticeships aren't really about teaching us how to do magic – more to help us understand what we have been doing all along. You'll learn the messy, medicinal side of being a witch, the importance of going around the houses[3], as well as how to avoid situations getting to a point where you actually need to do magic.

It's ALL messy, and that's why most of us wears black.
– E. Weatherwax

Witches need to be able to stick with and endure tough situations, which is why if you leave an apprenticeship without permission, no other witch will take you on. Though there are exceptions. One Ramtops witch was so strange and fearsome that apparently even if you left her after a single day, another place would be found for you and no one would say anything about it.

During my own training I stayed with a few witches, each with very different skills and specialisms, which helped me become the witch I needed to be. My first apprenticeship was with Miss Constance Level – a research witch. Miss Level taught me about the Doctrine of Signatures, a school of thought which states that plants and herbs give you clues as to what they can treat by

3. *See* Going Around the Houses. *Page 25*

You'll likely spend a lot of time picking and drying herbs

Mistress Pullunder's Luck of Lancre Silver Saddle (Erwin), a prize-winner

resembling the parts of the body where that ailment is suffered.[4]

After Miss Level, I spent some time with both Mistress Pullunder and Old Mother Dismass. Mistress Pullunder also focused on research and experimentation and taught me a lot about soil enrichment through her experiments in pedigree earthworm breeding, as well as how to tune wind chimes to repel demons through harmonic dissonance. The main thing I learned from my short stay with Old Mother Dismass was never to play cards with someone who suffers from temporal confusion, and the patience and focus needed to maintain a conversation with someone who was either hearing me in the previous week or answering something I'd ask the following month.

Miss Eumenides Treason, the fourth witch I was apprenticed to, specialized in Justice and was also an expert in borrowing.

4. *See* Research Witches. *Page 35*

Looka tha sise a tha scunner! Yes cud ride it into battle! — Rob

She went blind at sixty years old, and deaf at seventy-five, but it was never a trouble to her as she used the eyes and ears of any nearby animals to see and hear. She taught me about boffo, which is a kind of headology based around playing up to peoples' expectations to earn respect. I left when she had The Call, which meant her steading had to be allocated to another witch.

Next was Nanny Ogg, who lives in the least witchy house you can imagine, right in the centre of town. She wasn't officially my teacher, but you can't help learning things from her. What Nanny doesn't know about midwifery isn't worth knowing, but what she taught me most about was the power of listening. She can listen so hard that you find yourself telling her things you didn't even know you knew. Miss Treason referred to her as a strumpet. I looked this up and it means 'a woman of easy virtue'. Someone to whom virtue comes easily was obviously an excellent teacher. She knows all the old, dark stuff – the magic built into people and the landscape, which is only remembered as superstitions about touching wood and not walking under black cats. She taught me about folk memory, which is deep and dark and breathing and never fades. I learned the old rituals, like getting married by jumping over a fire together and even used it to marry Baron Roland and Letitia Keepsake.

Nanny's most powerful magic is in the way she's instantly at home and a part of everyday life anywhere she goes. People trust her and feel at ease with her in a way I'm not sure any other

And some of those things you might want to unlearn!
– E. Weatherwax

Hah!

Knowing how to marry a couple in a hurry can be very useful if there's a chance the bride might drop a tiny extra guest during the ceremony! Thankfully our Jason hung on until the reception. He's always loved parties!
– Nanny Ogg

Gytha 'Nanny' Ogg
and her cat Greebo

witch has ever managed – I hope one day I'll be even half as good with people as she is.

While I was never an official apprentice to her, Mistress Weatherwax gave me the confidence I needed to start my training. She gave me my first hat (an invisible one) and taught me what it means to be a witch. I learned that everything she does and says is some form of test. I hope I passed those tests, and that I live up to her example.

The Allocation of Steadings

Being known as the Bad Ass Witch certainly helped Esme's reputation along in the early days.
– Nanny Ogg

When a country witch has finished her training she will eventually take on a steading of her own. A steading is the <u>area</u> and population we are responsible for looking after. Sometimes witches inherit a cottage and steading from the witch who trained them, but if a witch dies and there is no one ready to take over, boundaries are redrawn to split the steading between neighbouring witches. Witchcraft is starting to become a little more popular again, hence me writing this book, so there are often several witches waiting for a cottage and steading to come up – and witches typically live for a long time, out of stubbornness as much as good health!

Proposals for who will inherit a steading are usually put forward by senior witches over a <u>good buffet</u> at the funeral of

Always keep a string bag about your person for leftovers, and remember, you can grab the best leftovers at the start of the buffet!
– Nanny Ogg

The Chalk,
my own steading

the soon-to-be deceased[5] witch. I'd like to say that steadings are awarded to the young witch who shows the strongest combination of promise, skill and attitude towards hard work, but at Miss Treason's funeral I realized that decisions are sometimes influenced by devious machinations and

I'm sure I have no idea what you're talking about!
- E. Weatherwax

5. *Witches get The Call, the knowledge they're going to die, a day or two in advance. Some choose to hold the funeral early so that they don't miss out on a good party.*

one-upmanship. When witch politics and egos come into play it can result in choices that may seem terrible at the time. However, no matter how much a witch rubs others up the wrong way, it's not good for any of us if one of us fails. So, we do what must be done and help each other out for the sake of witchcraft itself, *even if we never even get a thank you for it.*

I think a few unintentional words may have spilled out of your pen here.
— Miss Tick

HIERARCHY & SISTERHOOD

Whilst wizards have a clear hierarchy and a head wizard, as in the Unseen University's Archchancellor, things aren't nearly so clean-cut with witches. Most will tell you that we're all equal and the idea of a <u>leader</u> is against the spirit of witchcraft, but that's not the whole truth. There's definitely a pecking order based on age, respect and ability. The dominant personalities at the top will peck down hard at any witches who try to push their way past. Sometimes a young witch who hasn't proven herself yet might try to lord it over her peers. These upstarts are usually knocked down a peg or two when they have to roll up their sleeves and

Absolutely! Mistress Weatherwax would never allow that sort of thing. — Miss Tick

accept that witchcraft isn't all about silly incantations and looking good in a black dress and silver jewellery *although, annoyingly, that seems to work for SOME people!*

The collective name for a group of witches is an argument, which is what happens whenever a group of us get together. The older witches often refer to each other as sisters. This is actually very fitting. Having plenty of sisters myself, the fact that some witches are always bossing the younger ones about, vying for position and playing mind games with each other, feels pretty sisterly to me. Whenever I fell out with my sisters Hannah or Fastidia, we'd be so coldly polite to each other at the table that Dad would say he needed to put on a scarf and gloves just to sit and eat his dinner. That's nothing compared to elder witches. They're as polite as duchesses when they don't like each other. You'd lose a limb to frostbite if you walked between them when they were greeting each other.

Head Witch

No witch will admit there's such a thing as a head witch, but Mistress Weatherwax, Granny to her friends, is well known to be that witch. Even the Nac Mac Feegle call her the hag o' hags and there's not a mountain troll or wolf that will dare attack her when she's alone in the forest. Very few can come close to her in the feats she has achieved. She can share the mind of any

Of course you wouldn't have anyone in particular in mind there, Tiff?
— Nanny Ogg

She cud mak a Feegle cry 'Crivens!' and widdle his kilt from a mile awa!
— Rob

Mistress
Weatherwax,
Magrat Garlick
and Nanny Ogg

An' I wasn't the last, though I never thought of winnin' a frying pan.
- E. Weatherwax

animal,[1] even swarms of bees! Nanny tells me that she defeated the Queen of the Elves; put King Verence II on the Lancre throne and even took down her own sister who was destroying the kingdom of Genua. I thought it was just a rumour, but Queen Magrat told me that when a family of vampires tried to turn Mistress Weatherwax, she ended up infecting them instead, leaving them thirsting for tea instead of blood.
So, while we don't have a head witch, I'm glad it's Mistress Weatherwax, and that she's on our side!

Covens

Other than for the Witch Trials, you don't see more than a couple of witches together unless they really can't avoid it, but younger witches tend to be a bit more social so covens do spring up now and then. It's old fashioned to think that they need to be made up of three witches, Maiden, Mother and ~~Crone,~~ *the other one* and no matter how old she is no witch wants to be the crone. Even the word 'coven' isn't used that much, except in books that spell magic with a 'K'. Where I grew up everyone thought that witches danced around on moonlit nights without their drawers on, but I've been told that's optional.

When I first started out, I was invited into a coven made up of all the young witches in the area. There were eight of us and it was chaotic and a bit silly at first, with talk of 'opening the circle' and

Fun though. As long as you know where all the nettles and thistles are, and keep an eye out for sudden hedgehogs!
- Nanny Ogg

1. *See* Borrowing. *Page 68*

My first coven

I would hope your coven members are clear that the world is a disc! I'll be sure to direct the travelling teachers up to the Ramtops sometime.
– Miss Tick

'summoning the world's four corners' before we even did anything. We didn't dance around without our drawers on, but we did share news, warn each other about potential trouble, and talk about what we'd been learning on our various apprenticeships. It was quite nice to spend time with other witches around my age, and we've learned to support each other when needed – even helping those who act like they're doing you a favour by letting you support them.

Older witches don't bother so much with covens, but they do occasionally pay each other visits. If a witch spends too long on her own her thoughts can turn dark, and that's dangerous in someone with power. Checking in on each other now and then helps ensure that no one has started going to the bad.[2]

2. *See* Cackling. *Page 172*

(From left to right)
Dimity Hubbub,
Petulia Gristle,
Lucy Warbeck,
Gertruder
Tiring,
Lulu Darling
&
Harrieta Bilk

Missing:
Annagramma
Hawkins. I asked
everyone to
make sure to tell
Anagramma the
date they were
supposed to pose
for Mister Kidby,
but it appears every
single one of them
'forgot.

The Witch Trials

Back in my day we met in a meadow somewhere ourselves, just witches. Now it's all fun and games for the family.
— E. Weatherwax

Then maybe a handful of us should just meet in a meadow next year, instead of the trials?
— Nanny Ogg

Now, I didn't say I wanted to deprive the kiddies of a show.

The Lancre Witch Trials are where the witches of the Ramtops come together to catch up on gossip and demonstrate magical feats under the guise of friendly competition. It's a really big event. Hundreds of witches come from far and wide, and even ordinary folk come along for a <u>family day out</u>. There are food stalls, a fair and sideshows like the ones you get at agricultural

The Lancre
Witch Trials

shows down on the Chalk – Roll-a-penny, Lucky Dip, Bobbing
for Piranhas. There's also plenty of places to buy fancy witch
attire and magical equipment like dream catchers, pretty
shambles and self-emptying curse-nets – though watching
witches buy them is a bit like watching fish buy umbrellas!

The trials themselves take place in a roped-off square in the centre of the field. When volunteers are called for, any witch young or old can get up to perform a piece of magic and show what they can do and what they are becoming. They say that there are no judges, no prizes, no winners – and if you believe that you'll believe anything! Despite the fact no winner is ever announced, it is almost always Mistress Weatherwax, to the point where other witches have even petitioned her not to take part. Even if there's only the chance of winning a runner-up position, the trials are an excellent opportunity for young witches to demonstrate their skills in front of hundreds of their peers. A well-conducted magical feat earns respect, as Petulia Gristle learned when she performed the Pig Trick at the Witch Trials with only a sausage.

Brings back a memory.
~~...............~~
~~...............~~
~~...............~~
~~...............~~
~~...............~~
~~...............~~
~~...............~~
— *Nanny Ogg*

An artist's impression of Petunia Gristle's Pig Trick – rather less distressing than the real thing

Absolutely not.
– E. Weatherwax

The Currency of Respect

One of the first things Mistress Weatherwax ever said to me was 'I show you respect, as you in turn will respect me.' Respect is the most important thing any witch can possess, and even witches who aren't liked can still be greatly respected. Even the Nac Mac Feegle respect witches, though that doesn't stop them from calling us hags. True respect usually comes once you're an established witch with your own cottage, but you can work at earning it earlier.

Back when I was eleven and starting out as an apprentice to Miss Level, Mistress Weatherwax gave me leave to call her Granny.[3] Not only that, but during the Witch Trials she gave me her very own hat. I didn't immediately realize just how much she did for me that day, but from then on I had respect from all of the other trainee witches, and many of the older ones too. It gave me the strength I needed to go up against the Wintersmith, the Cunning Man, and the lords and ladies of Fairyland.[4] Respect is power. It is the most valuable currency we have and, in most cases, the only one we need.

> It's meat and drink to a witch.
> Without respect, you ain't got a thing.
> - E. Weatherwax

3. *Though in these pages I believe she deserves the respect of her full title, Mistress Weatherwax.*

4. *See On Gods, & Other Monsters. Page 136*

Nanny
Anapple

THE COUNTRY WITCH

Once a potential witch becomes apprenticed to an established witch with her own cottage and steading, it's time to learn what witches actually do every day. This probably won't be what you'd expect, and certainly wasn't what I expected. It's hard work and barely involves magic at all – at least not what you might think of as magic. Mistress Weatherwax said that witchcraft is mostly about doing quite ordinary things, and she was right – much of our role is about as ordinary as it gets. You're there, you have the hat, you do the job. The basic rule of witchery is: it's up to you.

Going Around the Houses

The villagers within our steadings look to us for medical advice, midwifery, conflict resolution, and jars of ointment, lotions and potions for aches, pains and various personal uses. Very early on in our training we start 'going around the houses'. There are always patients who need our care, new and expectant mothers to help and advise, and elderly widowers with toenails to cut. [1]

Miss Level called this 'filling what's empty and emptying what's full' but Granny Aching said it best; 'Feed them as is hungry, clothe them as is naked, speak up for them as has no voices.' That pretty much sums up our daily duties as witches, though I'd add; grasp for them as can't bend, reach for them as can't stretch, wipe for them as can't twist.

Going around the houses isn't just about caring for the sick and needy. It helps us keep a finger on the pulse of what's going on and spot those who haven't asked for help but might desperately need it; the woman who walks into doors too often, the teenage girl trying to hide her growing bump, the old man who spends his days alone in his chair, waiting for a visit from a son who died years ago. Make note of these things. Listen to the old men and women who want and need to talk. Keep your eyes open for what people are trying to hide, and your ears open for spill

For very personal problems, try my Chocolate Delight with Special Secret Sauce. You can find the recipe in my own book: The Joye of Snacks, bye a Lancre Witch.

— Nanny Ogg

An' just be clear WHJCH Lancre witch wrote that book! J ain't havin' people blamin' me for Banana Soup Surprise. Disgustin', Gytha Ogg!

- E. Weatherwax

---

1. *Wear eye protection. I've seen toenails smash through windowpanes!*

words. A witch learns more from <u>what people don't say</u> than from the words that actually leave their lips.

You will hear gossip all around you – always pick up more than you pass on. Think about what people say and how they say it, and watch their eyes. It's like a big jigsaw, but you're the only one who can see all the pieces – the only one looking to put them all together and see the reality. That's why we go around the houses, why we become part of people's lives, so that we can leave the lives we touch just a little bit better. Mistress Weatherwax always said the start and finish of witchcraft is helping people when life is on the edge. <u>Even people you don't like.</u>

The spill words I've heard could fill a book. One you'd have to keep in a vat of ice water to stop it sizzling!
— Nanny Ogg

That's it. That's the root and heart and soul and centre of it all.
– E. Weatherwax

Miss Treason's skulls

Conflict Resolution

As country witches, we're the ones people turn to when there are disputes or conflict within our steadings. It may be frustrating to get home exhausted only to be asked to pass judgement on piglet ownership after Widow Tockley's pig gave birth on Reg Bleakley's land, but we must hear the argument and deliver our verdict. It shows that we are respected and that our word is valued.

The disputes you'll deal with pretty much always involve land and livestock. On the Chalk, Granny Aching was the first person people turned to for conflict resolution. The old Baron himself once asked for her help, pleading mercy for his dog after it killed a sheep. Granny saved the dog from death by putting it in a barn with a fiercely protective ewe and her newborn lamb. It never looked at a sheep again. People thought it was witchcraft. It was really just an old shepherd's trick, but it doesn't mean it's not magic just because you know how it's done.

Aye, she was a witch all right. An one I'd very much like to have met.
— E. Weatherwax

While we all have to pass judgement from time to time, Miss Treason actually specialized in Justice. She would sit blindfolded at her click-clacking loom, lit by candles sitting on two skulls marked ENOCHI and ATHOOTITA (GUILT and INNOCENCE), as people laid out their problems. Then, the loom would stop dead. She'd take off her blindfold and stare through them with her pearly grey eyes as she delivered judgement. She was such a master of boffo – the art of appearance and meeting expectations – that no one dared argue with anything she said. Confidence and appearance are important if you want respect, and Miss Treason gave them the full show.

I reckon I know the ones. Page 8 of the Boffo catalogue?
— Nanny Ogg

I've learnt that a witch mustn't let people see her being unsure of herself, it makes them uncomfortable. Sometimes there is no right answer to a problem, no perfect solution other than banging two people's heads together. Just be as fair as you can be, and deliver your answer so confidently there can be no doubt in your verdict, or, like Miss Treason, be so fearsome that no one will ever dare question it!

A typical 'payment'

Compensation

I'm embarrassed to write the words, but when I first started going round the houses with Miss Level, I actually asked her if she stopped helping people who were too mean to pay. She told me that a witch never expects payment, never asks for it and just hopes she never needs to. Her words often ring in my ears, 'You can't not help people just because they're stupid or forgetful or unpleasant. Everyone's poor round here. If I don't help them, who will?' Back then I didn't understand why anyone would work without payment, or how we were supposed to get by without it – I was thinking about it all wrong.

I soon learned that a witch rarely needs to be concerned with money. Even cottages are passed down to us when we're ready to take on a steading of our own.[2] We get by with payment in kind – hand-me-downs, gifts, favours and appreciation for services. We're given clothing, free handiwork and more food than we can ever eat. Miss Level taught me to pass on what I don't need or can't use to those going through a bad patch, or who don't have anyone else to help them. She called it storing food in other people. It creates a cycle of people doing favours for each other, which keeps going round and everything just sort of… works!

2. *See* The Allocation of Steadings. *Page 12*

A challenge I am prepared to accept! Even those wriggly things in jars that Widower Arnold used to give us?

The ones that made noises at night? Okay, maybe not those.

Miss Constance Level

Also Miss Level

SPECIALIST WITCHES

As discussed in the previous chapter, all witches have a range of everyday core skills. Some witches may choose to become specialists in one of these areas, e.g. Miss Treason specialized in Justice and adjudication, Miss Level is an excellent herbalist and Nanny Ogg is the Disc's greatest midwife. Mistress Weatherwax told me that Nanny even delivered the child of Time herself, but that I shouldn't mention it in case she gets too <u>big for her boots</u>. *I believes I said 'provocative boots'. – E. Weatherwax*

There are more unique things a witch might choose to specialize in, such as fairy godmothering and voodoo witchcraft, but I've never encountered any witches who practise those skills on the Chalk or the Ramtops. I've listed some of the specialisms I know most about, but a witch can always carve out a specialism of her very own.

You show me where it's writte a witch can't wea red boots and I'll show you a wizard's staff
on the end!
– Nanny Ogg

Miss
Perspicacia
Tick

Witchfinders

Some witches specialize in witchfinding. These witchfinders aren't anything like the murderous witch-hunters[1] who invent excuses to burn women at the stake. They are travelling witches who seek out those who are just starting to discover a talent for the craft. It isn't good to be a witch alone, so witchfinders make sure any potential witches they find have the option to train with a mentor when they are old enough.

Witchfinding is considered a rather dangerous specialism as it takes you into places that can be very hostile to witches. Miss

1. *See* Witch-hunters. *Page 168*

Tick earmarked my friend, Lucy Warbeck, as a potential witchfinder and provided her with this great list of useful skills and tips for aspiring witchfinders:

- Always carry a piece of string and something living for shamble-making.[2]
- Study the making of, and more importantly untying of, all types of knot.
- Learn to swim, or wear heavy-enough boots to walk underwater.
- Practise holding your breath for a long time, or keep a hollow breathing reed in your boot.
- Always store a dry set of clothes and underwear near potential ducking ponds.
- Construct a stealth hat[3] with a retractable point.
- Don't carry matches. They just give people ideas if you're caught!

I recommend using a bit of transference if anyone tries to set a witch on fire. Give 'em a taste of their own flames!
— E. Weatherwax

I hope you wasn't cackling when you dictated that, Esme!
— Nanny Ogg

2. See Shambles. Page 72
3. See Hats. Page 46

A typical crystal ball

ZANTAX STRONGINTHEARM'S
MAGICAL EMPORIUM
LOVELY TO LOOK AT
· NICE TO HOLD ·
IF YOU DROP IT YOU
GET TORN APART BY
WILD HORSES

Enterprising Witches

While country witches get by due to the locals knowing the importance of looking after the witch who looks after them, in the big towns and cities money is a necessity. The witches there have to be far more enterprising to get by. There are various ways an enterprising witch can earn a living. Fortune-telling is a popular trade, as long as you give people the kind of fortunes they want to hear rather than any grim realities. There is also the option of medical work, treating patients who want a bit more discretion, such as the city watchmen or the local seamstresses.[4] Quite a few witches run pop-up stalls that sell ointments and

4. In case you're wondering why a seamstress would need confidential treatment for needle or scissor-related injuries, Nanny tells me 'seamstress' is actually a code word for 'ladies of negotiable affection'.

True fortune-telling could perhaps be more accurately named 'misfortune-telling'. However, while telling people about their impending misfortunes may be far more accurate and truthful, any witch doing so is unlikely to attract repeat custom.
— Miss Tick

potions with names like Maiden's Prayer and Husband's Helper.
Eskarina Smith, the first female wizard, told me that Mistress
Weatherwax even experimented in small-business ownership
when they travelled to Ankh-Morpork together. Apparently she
told fortunes and sold herbal remedies, potions, medicines and
charms from her lodgings in The Shades of Ankh-Morpork.
This was key to covering their financial expenses while Esk tried
to get into the Unseen University to start her training.

By far the most enterprising witch I've ever met is Eunice
Proust. Mrs Proust is a city witch to the bone. She operates the
Boffo Novelty and Joke Emporium in Ankh-Morpork with her
sons, Derek and Jack. Witches all across the Unnamed
Continent, and probably beyond, know of Boffo through their
extremely popular mail-order catalogue. Boffo sells everything a
witch could need to help her meet people's expectations – fake
warts, cackle boxes, Hag-in-a-Hurry costumes and self-stirring
cauldrons. Mrs Proust designs and engineers the products in her
workroom below the shop. When I met her there, it looked as
though she was wearing one of the shop's most popular witch
masks. She kept asking if I saw the joke yet. I had to wait until I
was absolutely sure before I finally dared say it, but she wasn't
wearing a mask at all! Mrs Proust bases the terrifying witch
masks on her very own appearance, making her quite literally the
face of Boffo as well as the driving force behind it.

A warning for any soon-to-be former maidens using that one – always get the young man's name and address first! — Nanny Ogg

Queues down the street I had. - E. Weatherwax

Goodie Whemper

Research Witches

Research witchcraft is an ancient skill that focuses on finding new spells by figuring out how old ones were really done. Apparently, the only reason why old spells often don't work is because the exact details have been lost to time. If such a recipe calls for toe of frog, a research witch will experiment to find out what type of frog, which specific toe[5] and the exact process required, right down to how many stirs of the cauldron are needed and which type of spoon to use.

5. *Miss Level never harms living animals. She only uses frogs that have died of natural causes, or suicide – Miss Tick told me frogs can get quite depressed at times.*

Miss Level takes the Doctrine of Signatures much further. She has discovered that plants that don't resemble body parts can still tell you exactly what they're to be used for if you know how to look. For example, some may bear written instructions that can only be viewed through a green magnifying glass by the light of a red cotton taper, and viewing the cut root of False Gentian by stored moonlight using a blue magnifying glass reveals the words

Good f4r Colds May cors drowsniss
Do nOt oprate heavE mashinry.[6]

I can't be havin' with that sort of thing. Rots the brain.
- E. Weatherwax

Research witches are voracious <u>readers,</u> which is highly unusual for a witch, and they always write things down. Queen Magrat of Lancre told me that her mentor, <u>Goodie Whemper,</u> was an expert research witch who left a whole library of books detailing her meticulous and highly accurate research. For example, if you've ever thrown an apple peel behind you and it didn't reveal the name of your intended, it's because you didn't use an unripe Sunset Wonder picked three minutes before noon on the first frosty day of autumn and peel it left-handedly with a silver blade less than half an inch wide.

Maysherestinpeace
— Nanny Ogg

Research witches are patient, methodical and burn with a huge and insatiable curiosity. However, it pays to temper your curiosity. As good a witch as she was, it was one research project too far when <u>Goodie</u> conducted an experiment to see how many bristles she could pluck from her broomstick, mid-flight, before it failed to stay aloft.

Maysherestinpeace

6. *Daisies aren't particularly good at spelling.*

My own dear Granny Aching

Veterinary Witches

A Pig Witch might not sound like something you'd aim to be in the craft, especially if you've read *To Ride a Golden Broomstick* by Letice Earwig. However, witches who can work wonders with sick livestock are valued and respected by people from miles around *far more so than those who waste time talking about higher magiK and waving crystal-encrusted wands*. My friend Petulia trained under Old Mother Blackcap, a respected pig-borer, cow-shouter and all-round veterinary witch. Petulia became particularly good with pigs herself, rising to fame locally with her public demonstration of the Pig Trick – using only a sausage. Anyone who has heard a pig in the transition stage between live pig and sausages would know the value of an expert pig-borer. Petulia can sit down with a pig and talk to it so gently and calmly about incredibly boring matters that the pig gives a happy yawn and enters an eternal sleep. That's the kind of magic that is *really* valued in the country.

I'm pretty sure my Granny Aching was a veterinary witch. She knew more about sheep than even sheep know. She never gave up on a single member of her flock and could revive lambs that anyone else would have given up for dead. I never heard her curse anyone, but she cussed the air blue at shearing time. The only mysterious potion she ever made was her Special Sheep Liniment, but it's so powerful that even a drop is enough to get the <u>Nac Mac Feegle</u>, the most violent and rebellious of all fairy races, to do your bidding.

When Granny Aching died, the Chalk suffered an incursion of creatures from a world known as Fairyland. They sensed that the barrier between our world and theirs was no longer so well protected. I realize now that not only was Granny a veterinary witch, she was an edge witch too. One so powerful that just her presence on the Chalk kept its people safe.

Little buggers we always raiding m still for scumble, but I reckon it's like lemonade to them compared to yer Granny's liniment.

— Nanny Ogg

Scumble gud 4 bairns, but liniment puts hairs on yer hairs!

— Rob

MRS LETICE EARWIG
HIGHER MAGIK, PROFESSIONAL SPELLS

Whilst a reasonable summarization of the areas in witches may choose to specialize, this chapter has completely neglected High Witches — those of us destined to follow the path of the higher MagiKs and pass on our teachings. A high witch does not mumble in hedgerows, arbitrate between fools, or potter around town drinking tea and cutting the toenails of the elderly. We feel the magiK of the universe fill our veins and guide us in pursuit of the Great Mysteries. We follow the wisdom and ways of the ancients. We use magical tools crafted for their specific purpose and when we perform magiK it is with strictly observed ritual and respect. Higher witchcraft is both science and religion. It is not tea and toenails.

Edge Witches

The first time I met the old kelda of the Chalk Hill clan, she told me that Granny Aching had guarded the edges and the gateways and that this duty was now mine. There are far more edges than most people know. The boundaries between life and death, this world and the next, night and day, right and wrong – it's our job to look to them. All of them. I guess I've been guarding the borders since I first wielded a frying pan against Jenny Green-Teeth and Queen Nightshade of Fairyland. We stand on the edge, where the hardest decisions are to be made, and we make those decisions so that others don't have to. We help the dying to find the door that will take them beyond pain and suffering. We protect our world from those who would destroy it. We balance on the knife edge of morality, sometimes doing the wrong things to ensure the right outcome.

To be an edge witch you must be sharp, even suspicious. You need to think fast and keep an eye on the way you think. You must be brave, but that doesn't mean you <u>shouldn't have fear.</u> They say witches are selfish, that we think of everything as ours – the land, even the people. That might be true, but we'll fight like hell to protect what belongs to us.

Bravery without fear is just stupidity.
– E. Weatherwax

Mistress Weatherwax,
a formidable edge
guardian

WITCH ATTIRE & ACCESSORIES

I f you grew up with older siblings, you will undoubtedly be familiar with attire that has been taken in, let out and passed down through the ages so many times that it feels like part of the family.

For me it was the blue dress. Harebell blue when it got to me, although my sisters swear that it was once a deep inky navy like the sky during a harvest moon. Family myth and rumour aside, that dress served me well; surviving fairy bites, my little brother Wentworth's near-constant stickiness and baby Feegle snot. So firstly, when it comes to witchly apparel, do not neglect what you already have. Even if many people have had it before you.

Whether you choose to dress for practicality, or style, or somewhere in between, appearance is important. It's not just about how you see yourself, but how the world sees you too.

Core dress

There are two schools of thought on how witches should clothe themselves – in black and in *literally* anything else. There's a lot to recommend about the classic black dress, or skirt and top combination. It doesn't show dirt, blood[1] or most common

1. *Yours or others.*

There's one school of thought. And this is the right one!
- E. Weatherwax

stains. And being a witch is often a messy business. You can go from mucking out goats to helping deliver a breech baby in barely the time it takes you to wash your hands. Black also mends well and looks good on pretty much anyone.

In short – you know where you are with black. It might be lacking in imagination, but given what a rigorous workout even the most basic of witching actually gives your imagination, some prefer to not waste it on their clothes.

My usual attire

Black Aliss

I've had enough of darkness. When I get old, I shall wear midnight, but for now I choose to embrace something a little less austere. And whilst you shouldn't be afraid of colour, assess it with a carefully raised eyebrow. Internal or otherwise. Remember you're probably a witch just starting out, and not the Amazing-Bonko-and-Doris. If small children start asking you to make balloon animals, then it may be time to tone it down a notch. Once you get a decade or two of witchcraft under your belt, feel free to notch it back up again.

Green can be nice. Especially if you live in an area where grass stains are commonplace. It's also the favoured colour of Queen

Magrat, part-time witch and occasional warrior woman. I have always considered her to be quite a progressive when it comes to attire, and the first witch I've met to ever wear <u>trousers</u>. I've never tried them myself, but my apprentice, Geoffrey Swivel, tells me that they are both comfortable and practical as witch attire.

And full-time wet hen!
— E. Weatherwax

Bifurcated!

Queen Magrat is also the only witch I know to have donned full armour, complete with spiked breastplate and a double-headed battle axe. Whilst wearing excessive amounts of heavy metal is not generally advised in a profession where being thrown in ponds or lakes is a risk, it's certainly memorable. So, don't be afraid to experiment. One day, you might find that a battle axe might be just what you need to complete your look. Not to mention a great problem solver.

Queen Magrat of Lancre in the time before her coronation

Everyone can see her legs.
No they can't, the material is in the way.
— Nanny Ogg
Yes, but they can see where her legs are.
Everyone's naked under their clothes.

I'm not, I got three vests on.

Hats

Perhaps the most important part of a witch's attire is the hat. People have a tendency to see that hat before they see the person beneath it. Although in my case, the first hat I was given couldn't be seen at all. It was an invisible hat given to me by Mistress Weatherwax. And although there was barely any weight to it, I could just see it shimmering in the air like a heat haze over my head. It made me feel like a witch even before I entered my training – an internal hat.

Bware pointy bonnets! – Rob

When it comes to physical hats, I've always favoured the classic pointy-and-black type. It confers authority, respect and does a lot of the mental heavy lifting for you. People see the hat and they instantly think 'witch!' This is one of the reasons the magic works, Mistress Weatherwax always says.[2] People talk to the hat more than they talk to me. Without it, I feel like I'm in disguise.

Mistress Weatherwax swears by making your own hat for that individual touch. But if you prefer to buy one, many witches recommend the ones made by Mr Vernissage in Slice who specializes in willow reinforcing and multiple internal pockets. Remember: A witch can never have too many pockets! Nanny Ogg has a hat from Mr Vernissage that she believes 'stops 100% of all known farmhouses'. I wouldn't have thought that there was much of a risk of having a farmhouse dropped on your head, but since the number is definitely more than zero, you may wish to

No hat like the one you make yourself. – E. Weatherwax

2. See Headology. *Page 62*

Still happy to give my official approval Mr Vernissage. Yous knows my address. – Nanny Ogg

factor this into your purchasing decisions.

Of course, there may be circumstances where people thinking 'witch!' because of the hat is the last thing you want. There are still places where it's best for a witch to pass by unnoticed. Miss Tick has a special 'stealth' hat for just such an occasion, which can turn from being an innocuous flat straw hat, complete with straw flowers, to a pointy black one in the literal flick of a switch.

Patent pending!
— Miss Tick

Another potential stealth hat is an edible one. On a trip to Genua, Mistress Weatherwax was gifted a fruit-based hat by the legendary voodoo witch Erzulie Gogol. Most of the evidence that such a hat existed was daiquiried-away by Nanny. But there's a fig tree in her garden that grows very fast and produces the best fruit you've ever tasted. I very much hope to visit Genua one day and meet Mrs Gogol. Anyone who can get Mistress Weatherwax to put a pineapple on her head must be a powerful witch indeed.

Whilst Nanny Ogg and Hilta Goatfounder have been known to embrace fake fruit as a hat accessory, you need to be a witch of some standing to carry this off. Nanny only really uses her wax-cherry hat when attending family feuds. Granted these are feuds that she's usually started. Letice Earwig, who believes there is no such thing as over-advertising when you're a witch, likes to add silver stars to her hat. But then there's not much that she doesn't like to add silver stars to. Whilst not one for decorating her hat, Lucy Warbeck often uses hers to hide the knife and fork she has stuck into her hair-bun, which is undoubtedly one of the more unusual looks.

Lies, Tiff! I just nudge them along a bit.
— Nanny Ogg

Since we never knows when a free meal might be heading our way I call this practical

ZAKZAK STRONGINTHEARM'S

MAGICAL EMPORIUM

THE TWISTED SISTER

THE RUNE SLINGER

THE SKYSCRAPER

THE CLOUDBURSTER

THE COUNTRYWOMAN

THE SAFETY

ZakZak
Stonginthearm's hats
are as much fashion as
function

ZAKZAK STRONGINTHEARM'S
MAGICAL EMPORIUM

THE SOOTHSAYER

THE CRYSTALGAZER

THE TAINTED VEIL

THE THUNDERHEAD

THE MYSTIC LOCK

Cloaks

It's also advisable to invest in a cloak early on. A good cloak can also have a multitude of uses when not being worn, such as a goat blanket, fruit collector and emergency tent. There are many fancy cloaks out there that can turn a young witch's head. Some, such as those made by wizard tailors, can be imbued with their own magic – with the consistency of smoke, and the warmth of a Feegle mound. But not every witch suits every cloak. So be aware of who you are, and more importantly who you are not. You may feel like you're conveying a sense of <u>elegance and mystery,</u> but to the outside world you probably look like you're trying to navigate your way through your own personal hurricane.

Gravitarse!
– E. Weatherwax

Cloaks can also keep others warm

Granny
Weatherwax's
boots

Boots

Whilst a witch's hat might get them into trouble, a witch's boots
will help get them out of it. Make sure they're solid, with a
thick sole, hobnails and crescent-shaped scads. Tough enough
to administer a good kick when needed, durable enough to deal
with tough terrain and inclement weather, and light enough for
ease of running away or jump-starting an errant broomstick.
I have an aversion to brand new boots as I like to feel that my
footwear is used to working for a living. A bit of polish to keep
the weather out is fine, but a witch's boots should not shine.

Black and brown are the traditional colours, but Nanny
Ogg has also experimented with red leather boots. As with

Nanny's red boots. I'm not sure what people say about women who wear red boots, but Nanny assures me it's all true.

Mistress Weatherwax, what Nanny Ogg can get away with is not necessarily what the rest of us can get away with. You need a certain amount of natural Oggishness to pull off red boots. Oggishness is a quality that is often underestimated by the witching world. But what can seem like naive friendliness and bumbling affability, is actually the kind of charisma that encircles you like a serpent and, before you know it, has rendered you helpless. It's a true power indeed. If you're close enough to smell the tobacco, then she's already got you. So, if you are lucky enough to have one, don't neglect your inner Ogg.

And if you live nearby don't neglect your outer Ogg either. All cakes, pies and ales gratefully received.

— Nanny Ogg

Undergarments

And thinking about Oggishness, this is definitely one area of witch attire I can hear Nanny Ogg sniggering about. But it's certainly an item of clothing that I wish I'd considered more thoroughly in the early days. Not only do undergarments make good emergency bandages in a pinch but, like cloaks, they are a must for broomstick travel. On chilly nights, you will need several pairs. I suggest using wool ones as the outer layer only, never the inner one.

Me? Never! Bloomers can provide a very useful storage for buffet items. Just remember to remove them before more... intimate encounters. An avalanche of prawn vol-au-vents can really ruin a mood.

Ruined mine just reading that. ~ E. Weatherwax

Safety first, Hamish! ~ Rob

An aviatory treasure trove for flight-inclined Feegles

Jewellery

The type and quantity of jewellery you choose to wear is very much down to personal taste. Or sometimes lack of it. Hilta Goatfounder was said to wear so many bangles that she sounded like the percussion section of an orchestra falling off a cliff.

Many members of my first coven were fans of large amounts of occult jewellery. Annagramma Hawkin had the innate style to pull it off. Unsurprising, given that her first mentor was Letice Earwig, who wore so much silver that she looked like one of those shiny bird scarers.

I've never been clear about how much actual power occult jewellery actually grants its wearer. No doubt the belief that it does must count for something. A kind of self-boffoing. But there's definitely a tipping point where protection for the wearer can become hazardous. When I first met Petulia Gristle, you couldn't be in her company for more than a few minutes without having to untangle her from other bits of her. Bracelets from buttons, necklaces from hair, and even one time an earring from an ankle chain – no one is too sure exactly how that happened. She told me that they were for protection, but they didn't protect her from looking a bit silly. She wears fewer these days after getting her occult cuff caught in the bristles of a pig she was boring, and nearly getting crushed.[3]

It's not just birds that fly away when they see her coming.
– E. Weatherwax

3. *See Veterinary Witches. Page 37*

Hilta Goatfounder

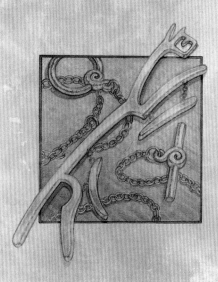

My first piece of jewellery certainly had a little magic about it. Although I wouldn't have called it occult. Something older than that. Earthy. A silver necklace in the shape of the white horse etched into the hillside of my Chalk home and given to me by Baron Roland when we were both younger and the world seemed… smaller. When I first saw the white horse as a child, it didn't really look like a horse to me. Just a collection of curvy lines. I asked my father about it and he told me what Granny Aching had told him, 'Taint what a horse looks like. It's what a horse be.' She was right. It's the speed, the movement, the essence of a horse. And when you know that you can finally see it.

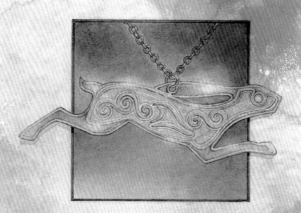

For me jewellery is there to remind you of a moment, a feeling or a piece of knowledge that you want to become part of you. That may only be for a few days, like the ring I had made from the nail heart of the Wintersmith. Or longer, like the gold necklace gifted to me by my dear friend, Preston – a golden hare running into the flames, to remind me to have courage to face my fears and find a way through them. Whether it's a hundred bangles, a little iron nail or a silver horse, find what speaks to you and speaks from you.

WITCH MAGIC

What surprised me most about witchcraft was realising that most witches can get through their whole lives without having to do what you might consider actual magic. Most witchcraft is practical medicine, headology, common sense and being the one willing to make a stand. I think we all start out in the craft expecting to be casting spells every day and to no longer need matches to light a fire, but that's wizard magic. Elder witches have told me that wizard magic comes from the sky. It's too showy – all lightning bolts, illusion, fireballs and throwing magic around just to see what happens. Witches don't use that sort of magic unless we really have to, and we very rarely have to. Our magic is different. It comes from the earth[1] and the elements. It doesn't need fancy equipment, ancient spell books or a full moon, though it never hurts to put on a bit of a show.

I must remind you that this is a guide to magic, not an instruction manual. I can tell you how to do magic, but not how *you* would do it. It's all about getting your mind right, and we all do that in different ways, just as we all access and perform magic differently. You'll need to find your own way to do any of the things described here, but if you're reading this book it's probably already in you. You just need to figure out how to let it out.

Wizards! Always hexperimenting! If that sort of magic was difficult, wizards wouldn't be able to do it.

– E. Weatherwa

1. Miss Tick firmly believes that the type of earth you live upon has an impact on a witch's magic. See The Power of the Land. Page 93

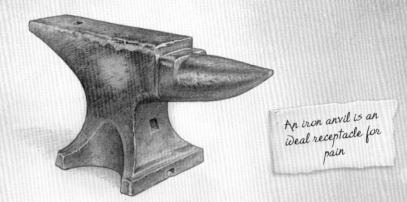

An iron anvil is an ideal receptacle for pain

Balance & Transference

Magic is all about balance – whether it's restoring balance, or being a balancing force. Witches must be like the centre of a see-saw – the place that never moves. We must be this force in our communities, but also maintain a balance within ourselves as we perform magic. If you have the perfect centre you can become a pivot, the point of stability in the transference of energy.

Mistress Weatherwax told me that magic is just moving stuff around. I first saw her demonstrate this when she transferred the heat from a cup of tea to my arm, leaving the tea as a lump of ice. I used that skill on a larger scale to channel the heat of a bonfire to melt huge snow drifts after a perpetual winter blanketed the Chalk in snow. You just have to practise. Get your mind right. Become the axis through which power flows so that it flows *through* you, not *into* you.

Transference also works with pain. With practice, you can transfer it to a place just outside your patient's body, even take it away with you. The more pain that is being suffered, the more careful you need to be as you work to remove it. A slip in concentration can cause it to escape, either going back into the patient all at once, or into you rather than passing through you – all of that pain in a single second. The best place to send it is into iron, such as an anvil – something that absorbs it rather than feels it. Mistress Weatherwax says that we don't feel the pain we take from others. That's not entirely true, but because it's not our pain it is much easier to carry.

Balance also applies to transforming things into other things. For various personal reasons, I have asked Miss Tick to talk about this.

Brian

You Don't Have to Be Magic to Work Here But it Helps!

Don't worry, Tiff. ZakZak Stronginthearm says Brian don't even remember the pink balloon.

— Nanny Ogg

Spare Brian

Transmogrification

As Tiffany wisely pointed out, balance must be considered in all things. People typically think witches go around turning people into frogs. We don't. Not because we don't occasionally feel the urge, but because of what wizards call 'conservation of mass'. Take amphibians as an example. Frogs are far smaller than people. So, to turn a human into a frog, you would either have to transform them into a frog of equal mass, or find something to do with all of the leftover bits. It is far easier to simply make someone believe that they are a frog.

Several years ago I had a talking toad as a travelling companion. I eventually learned that he was once a lawyer who was turned into a toad by an angry fairy godmother. His memory is rather foggy when it comes to the transmogrification itself, so I have a feeling that the parts surplus to requirement were irretrievably disposed of, meaning that were he to be transformed back into a human he would remain forever toad-sized.

Far more entertaining too! Esme, remember when you convinced Mr Wilkins you'd turned him into a frog?
— Nanny Ogg

Last time he ever called me a domineerin' ol' busybody!
- E. Weatherwax

Mrs Wilkins says he loves swimming now. And there's never a fly to be seen in the kitchen.

Frog Brian

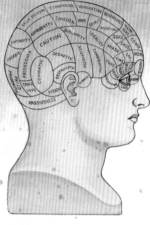

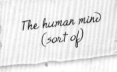

The human mind
(sort of)

Headology

A lot of magic is knowing things other people don't know. Things people don't understand can seem like magic, and sometimes it's easier to play upon their beliefs than try to explain a truth they don't understand or don't want to hear. This is headology. Not many witches use the word, which I believe was made up by Mistress Weatherwax, but they all practise it every day. It's a sort of psychology which takes advantage of what people already think and believe. It can heal aches and pains, get people to be nicer to each other, or cause them to change their ways entirely. Even our hats are headology. The hat is what sets us apart and gives people belief in our abilities.

I first saw Mistress Weatherwax using headology when we went around the houses together. At first I was uncomfortable. It seemed like she was just <u>lying to people,</u> but it actually helps them when an

You have to tell people a story they can understand. A story gets things done.
— E. Weatherwax

honest approach fails. For example, I tried a dozen times to explain to a family that their children were sick because their privy was too close to the well and contaminating their drinking water. They didn't listen. All Mistress Weatherwax had to do was tell them that the sickness was caused by goblins who were attracted to the smell of the privy and they started digging a new well immediately! She told someone else that his chest pains would go away if he walked to a waterfall each day and threw in three shiny pebbles for the water sprites. She was right, they did go away. But only because he was going for a five-mile walk every day, nothing to do with water sprites. Yet if I'd prescribed more exercise he wouldn't have listened at all. Rather than mocking their beliefs or trying to teach them lessons they don't want to learn, headology practitioners just use their patients' superstitions to get them to do what is best for them.

With headology, a witch doesn't have to curse someone to right a wrong. It's enough to smile at them a bit funny every time you see them and they will believe that everything bad that happens to them is the result of that non-existent curse until they make amends. If someone believes they're unlucky, you can mumble any magical-sounding words over a bottle of coloured water with herbs in it and give it to them as a luck potion. Just the fact that they believe in it will make them feel more lucky and, as a result, more confident and likely to bring luck their way. When using headology it helps to convey so much confidence in who you are and what you say that no one will doubt you. It is perhaps a witch's most powerful tool.

Boffo

Boffo is a lot like headology in that it plays up to people's expectations. I use it as a term to describe any form of reputation building through a bit of deceit. It's showing people what they want to see, what they expect rather than what is actually there. I got the name from a catalogue and merchandise from Boffo's Novelty and Joke Emporium, which I discovered in Miss Treason's cottage. Among its best customers are witches who wish they hadn't been cursed with clear complexions, excellent teeth and beautiful nails. Boffo offers a full range of cosmetics and prosthetics, such as rubber warts, green face-paint, stick-on claws and fake teeth, for the 'Hag in a Hurry'. They even have a home accessories range.[2] All of this terrifying window dressing really impresses locals who want a real witch worthy of nightmares, and gives them more faith in a witch's competence and power *even in those who rely on others to make them look competent.*

Boffo isn't just about the way that you present yourself, but also building your reputation through stories. Horrifying stories circulated about Miss Treason, who supposedly wore a clockwork heart, ate spiders, kept a demon in her cellar and would cut people's bellies open with her thumbnail if they'd been bad. It turned out she'd started most of the stories herself, then they took on a life of their own and new stories were born. Boffo created

2. See Boffo for the Home. *Page 90*

Be sure as to pass my respects to Miss Hawkin next time you sees her. I hear she's building quite a reputation for herself.

— E. Weatherwa

Mrs Eunice Proust

the illusion of a terrifying hag around a witch who, when you stripped it all away, was simply a disabled old lady. So, if you're having trouble gaining respect through youth, age or a wart-free complexion, don't be afraid to get a head start with boffo.

POPULAR PROSTHETICS
& ABHORRENT ACCESSORIES

HAIRY
WART SET
FREE
WITH EVERY ORDER

THE PLOUGH

Price .... AM$20

THE SUPERSONIC

Price .... AM$12

THE DARK NOSTRIL

Price .... AM$13

FOREST CONFECTIONER

Price .... AM$7

THE BEAK'D MEANACE

Price .... AM$9

LOATHSOME LOBES

ELDRITCH EARS

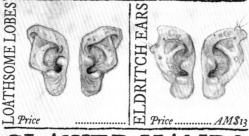

Price .... (LOATHSOME LOBES)

Price .... AM$13 (ELDRITCH EARS)

CLAWED HANDS

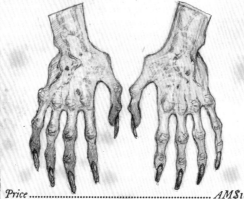

Price .... AM$13

THE TONGUE of TERROR

FUNGAL FEET

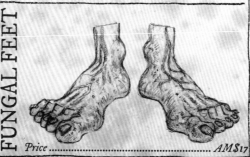

Price .... AM$17

DIABOLICAL DENTISTRY

THE HAG

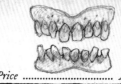

Price .... AM$6

THE CRONE

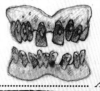

Price .... AM$7

THE BEDLAM

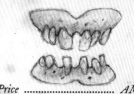

Price .... AM$7

THE SNAGGLE-TOOTH

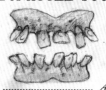

Price .... AM$8

THE TOMBSTONE

Price .... AM$9

!!!EXPEDITED RAIL DELIVERY NOW AVAILABLE!!!

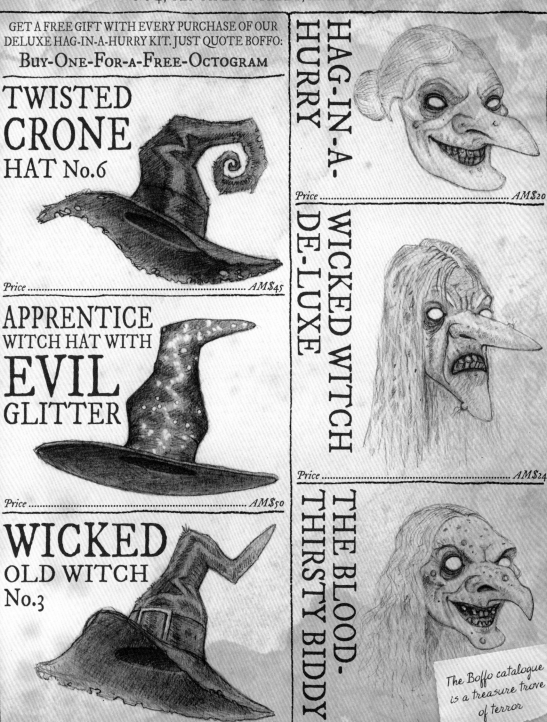

GET A FREE GIFT WITH EVERY PURCHASE OF OUR DELUXE HAG-IN-A-HURRY KIT. JUST QUOTE BOFFO: **BUY-ONE-FOR-A-FREE-OCTOGRAM**

TWISTED CRONE
HAT No.6

Price .... AM$45

APPRENTICE
WITCH HAT WITH
EVIL
GLITTER

Price .... AM$50

WICKED
OLD WITCH
No.3

Price .... AM$37

HAG-IN-A-HURRY

Price .... AM$20

WICKED WITCH DE-LUXE

Price .... AM$24

THE BLOOD-THIRSTY BIDDY

Price .... AM$28

The Boffo catalogue is a treasure trove of terror

Borrowing

Granny Weatherwax's sign, used to avoid misunderstandings

Borrowing is the ability to let your mind leave your body and enter the mind of another creature. Witches borrow mainly when they are searching for something, whether it's checking on the land around them or gathering information. The creature you are borrowing becomes your eyes and ears. This skill was very useful to Miss Treason who was blind and deaf but sent a little of her mind out into any creatures around her, using their eyes and ears to look and listen for her.

Apparently only one in a hundred witches can actually borrow. I discovered the first step by accident all because the mirror in my bedroom was too small and damaged for me to see myself properly. I figured out that I could just step outside of my body and see

myself. I called it 'See Me'. What I didn't consider was the fact that I was leaving my body unprotected, which led to it being possessed.[3]

I haven't wanted to share a mind with another creature since that experience, so I've asked Mistress Weatherwax, the most skilled witch at borrowing on the Disc, to write more about the practice.

(with thanks to Miss Tick for transcribing)

First, find somewhere comfortable and safe to lie down. Bed's best. I advise leavin' a note to let people know that you ain't dead, as your body will appear that way. To begin, let your mind wander. You'll start to feel the minds of creatures around you – the small fast minds of mice, the sharp minds of predators, even the earthworms deep in the soil. You'll hardly notice humans 'cos they're thinking so many things at the same time that it's like tryin' to nail fog to a wall. When you find a mind you want to borrow, enter with care. Don't upset the owner, it'll fight back or panic. Borrowing isn't about taking control of the mind you

This is meant literally. You need to find your own way to do it, but you just sort of let your consciousness expand and wander out of yourself.
– Tiffany

Aye, but it can soon become that way for some. There's many witches who've become lost in a mind and never returned. We've had to bury bodies that finally gave up on the ghost ever returning. I still leave out bacon rind for a bluetit that I'm sure was old Granny Postalute.
– Nanny Ogg

3. See An Open Mind. Page 166

enter — you work in harmony with it, suggestin' that it might be inclined to go one way or another. If you try to take over completely you will eventually lose yourself. Bear in mind that you've only been that creature for a brief sliver of time, but it has been itself for a lifetime.

When you master borrowing, an' I means really master it, you can find minds you didn't even know were there. You can reach into the soul of the land and feel its memories and strength, even its fears. Even buildings can have minds of sorts. The stones of the wizard university have so much magic in 'em that the building developed a personality. I borrowed it once, just for a moment. Stay long in a mind like that and you'd quite literally turn to stone.

Bees, now bees is the real test. All bees are part of a Livemind — The Swarm. When you're starting out with bees, you can send just a tiny bit of yourself out with them, a simple message or question in their minds that you want broadcasting to all hives. The Swarm can search the whole land within hours and return to tell you where to find what you need. But to truly borrow bees you must let your mind split into shards yet keep it whole, even when it's all flyin' out in different directions. You're looking out of all those eyes at once, seein' everything that they see, knowin' everything that they know. One mind with thousands of bodies, it's enough to send anyone cackling. You've got to be good to do it with bees.

Last thing I'll tell you, when you part minds from a creature you've borrowed, remember to show your gratitude by leaving some food out, and take only experience, leave nothing but memories.

Also remember you can't fly before opening any upstairs windows or stepping off cliffs!
— Nanny Ogg

Granny Postalute
...we think

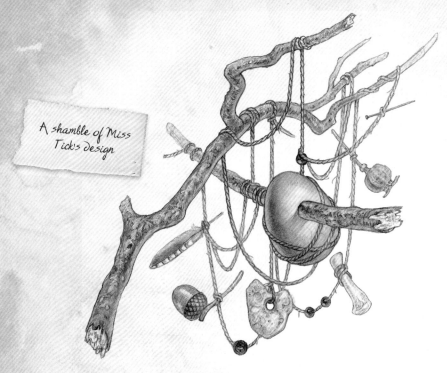

A shamble of Miss Tick's design

The Making of Shambles

A shamble is a swiftly assembled tool through which magic works. Shambles aren't magical in themselves but can be used for protection, to <u>detect magic and danger</u> around you, or even to amplify spells. If you've visited witchcraft stalls, like the ones at the craft fair in Slice, you've probably seen shambles on display – beautiful webs of string interwoven with feathers, beads, crystals and dried flower-heads. Though they're nice as decoration, those

Arts an' crafts. Fine for 'em as needs to start out on crutches, but if there's dangerous magic around a witch don't need no tools to find it, they feels it in their bones. Toys can just get in the way.
– E. Weatherwax

shambles are dead. They have either served their purpose, or were built with no other intention but to look pretty. In any case, a shamble must be made by you, and in the moment you need to use it.

I don't use shambles often so I've asked Miss Level to write about how to make them, as she was the witch who taught me.

Actually, Tiffany has already given you the key to making a shamble. It's all about the moment in which you are making it, and keeping your intention clear. After one of my apprentices struggled a lot with the process, I came up with an easier way to teach it. Just remember the three P's, Pockets, Purpose and Process, and you can't go far wrong.

— Miss Level

If it helps any other witches in training, I'm happy to admit that this was me. It's possible to fail by trying too hard when shamble-making. Miss Level's three P's should get you through it!

— Tiffany

Pockets

A shamble is made from whatever you have in your pockets at the time. While a witch should always carry a spool of thread or a long piece of string, it also helps to make sure you have the right sort of things in your pockets so that your shamble doesn't just contain keys, stray buttons and lint. I carry a few sequins to remind me of my circus days and I look out for interesting feathers, stones with holes in them, scraps of colourful cloth, beads and seed pods. Most importantly, a shamble must always contain something living. This is the most important element and will become the heart of your shamble. It could be a fresh egg, a beetle, even a passing snail. I once witnessed a Feegle parachute down from the sky to become the centre of a shamble under construction. A gesture that led to a shamble powerful enough to catch a hiver, and potential evidence that the more meaningful the elements of a shamble are to you, the more powerful it may be.

*A very interesting theory. One that I
would love to research further with you.*
— Miss Tick

Happy to help a hag oot! Rob

Purpose

At is important to hold in your mind the reason why you are creating a shamble. Some witches use them daily to paint a quick picture of what is going on around them and whether there's anything to worry about. Shambles can also be used like curse-nets to catch and contain harmful forces around you, or as a detector to find those forces or any other magic being performed nearby. Shambles can amplify spells you are casting, in which case think of yourself pulling back a bow as you create one. This will charge the device ready to send the spell further than you would have been able to cast it. Whatever the purpose, you must keep this at the forefront of your mind as you build your shamble.

Process

There isn't a great deal I can say
about the actual weaving of a shamble,
as your hands will take care of that
once you get your mind right. Stay
calm. Don't rush more than you need to.
Look at the shamble, see what's there,
but also notice the gaps where things
should be. What do you feel should be
there? Block out everything you don't
need, noise, fear, doubt – focus only on
the shamble and its purpose. Be in the
moment. As you achieve that state you
will find that everything becomes clear
and your hands will know what to do
– weaving the shamble into its perfect
form, showing you what you need to
see, telling you what you need to know,
protecting you from harm.

One of my few
successful shambles

The ink and water method

Scrying

If you believe everything anyone who spells magic with a 'K' tells you, you might think that you can't scry without expensive equipment. Fortunately, scrying is possible, and more effective, with simple things you can find cheaply, or just lying around the house. A glass fishing float does the same job as a crystal ball. The darker the surface the better the picture, so most witches find a few drops of black ink in a saucer of water to be the most effective scrying device. Again, I can't tell you exactly how to do it. You just sort of focus then listen with your eyes until the ink draws you in, like a long tunnel between you and what you want to see. Be aware that there are some places you will find impossible to scry into. These are places with a large build-up of unpredictable magic, like the magical waste heap outside of the Unseen University, and patches of gnarly ground.[4]

4. See The Power of the Land. *Page 93*

The Non-Use of Magic

Miss Tick told me that once you've learned everything you can learn about magic, then you've got the most important lesson still to learn – not to use it. Magic is difficult to control. It attracts the attention of things you didn't even know existed.[5] Even worse, you might slip into using magic for everyday things and become more and more disconnected from humanity and reality until one day you're cackling to yourself in your gingerbread cottage in the woods, or facing your sister witches on the battlefield. Magic has its place, but we must ensure that it keeps to it.

MRS LETICE EARWIG
HIGHER MAGIK, PROFESSIONAL SPELLS

I am, quite frankly, astonished by the lack of substance in this chapter. It claims to cover types of witch magic yet focuses almost entirely on folk magic and omits all types of ceremonial magiK. I see nothing on astral and celestial magiKs, or conjuration, ritual and chaos magiKs. Elemental magiK is touched upon but the harnessing of elements other than fire is mostly ignored. For a book on witchcraft to not even touch upon the importance of a book of shadows and the correct casting of a sacred circle raises great concern. I would implore any witch who wishes to become proficient in high magiK to turn immediately to my book *First Flights in Witchcraft*, followed by *To Ride a Golden Broomstick*.

5. See An Open Mind. Page 166

Flying high above the Chalk. Feegle not recommended.

EQUIPMENT

There are several items that you might expect a witch to possess when you first enter the craft, but you'll soon find that the only equipment a witch really needs is her hat. However, there are a number of things that can certainly come in very handy, and others that are not as essential as non-magical folk might think.

Broomsticks

I dreamed of flying long before I dreamed of being a witch. And once I learned about broomsticks, there was nothing I wanted more than to soar through the skies as free as a bird, or sail across the moon with an <u>entourage of bats</u> at my heels. 'Ah ha,' you're probably thinking, 'I bet she got that part about witchcraft wrong too!' And on a good day, I would take that bet because riding a broomstick is genuinely one of the most exhilarating parts of being a witch, at least once you get the hang of it and stop throwing up. But, as I'm sure you've now become aware, as with so many things around being a witch, it's a little more complicated than it may first appear.

Unless flying in Überwald, where I suggest a garlic necklace might be required to ward off those particular bats.
— Nanny Ogg

Solid broomsticks will often be hand-me-downs or spare brooms from other witches. Dwarfish craftsmanship is best. And due to Mistress Weatherwax being such a good <u>customer</u> of the Ramtop dwarfs, they have become the most reliable source of broomstick creation and repair in these parts. Always mention Mistress Weatherwax's name for a discount *and if you want to see a dwarf sweat from their beard*. I can also heartily recommend Shrucker and Dave's broomstick workshop under the railway arches in Ankh-Morpork. Ask how Shrucker's lumbago is doing and that might

And pretty much everything else!
— E. Weatherwax

Rubbish! Everything's better with garlic... aside from custard.

I ain't a customer. They hardly ever let me pay.

And sometimes they've been known to throw in a few bottles of broomstick oil just to get you out the door!

get you a free woodworm treatment.

I've never forgotten my first broomstick ride because the white-hot fear is seared into my memory. I was a passenger on the back of Miss Level's broomstick, travelling to her steading to start my first apprenticeship. We encountered turbulence early on and the broom dropped like a stone out of the sky. It halted just before hitting the ground and we then engaged in what Miss Level called 'hedge hopping'. This involved travelling a few feet above the ground and jumping every hedge or fence we came to, with the aerial grace of a water balloon. In fairness, Miss Level tried to put me at ease with lots of shouts of 'Upsadaisy!' or 'Here we go!' but it didn't really help and I was sick twice, which is where being closer to the ground was an unexpected benefit.

It took me a good while to get the hang of broomstick riding, so don't expect to be doing any soaring right away. I can recommend stabiliser sticks for those who need a little extra support. Folks may snigger, but not as much as they do if you wobble into a privet hedge. Stabilizer brooms are also good for carrying familiars in comfort, although I strongly advise against transporting Feegles as they have been known to set fire to the bristles.

Handy helf n' safety chek!
– Rob

Each broom is imbued with its own power, although it can take a while for it to kick in, so I suggest a running start to allow the magic to catch on to what's expected of it. Remember that your broomstick is the only thing between you and a sudden exposure to the ground, so treat it well. And always wear at least two pairs of undergarments – you will thank me.

String is one of the most useful things you can carry

Pocket Equipment

I've always been a big fan of pockets. And, in general, witches tend towards being extremely pocket-y people. There's not much that we won't try to put a pocket in. Even the invisible hat that Mistress Weatherwax gave me had pockets, but I never dared put anything in them. I've always found a piece of string to be one of the most useful bits of pocket equipment, whether you're a witch or not. Add in a few coins, a small knife and a snack and you're pretty much set for most minor adventures.

However, witches need to have a few more bits and pieces on hand for all eventualities. Bottles of coloured water are useful if you need an immediate 'cure' for something when practical advice alone hasn't worked – remember that sometimes the story is more effective than the actual remedy. If you're a travelling witch, breathing reeds can be kept in longer, internal pockets, or tucked into boots. If you find yourself being thrown into a river, pond or lake, these will become your new best friend.

Items that can be used to make a shamble are essential – anything interesting you find along the way will do, as long as you're drawn to them. Items with holes in or those that can be quickly tied together work best. A shamble always needs something living, so some witches carry insects in matchboxes about their person. Given the unpredictable nature of a witch's life, I find this to be a little cruel, aside from Petulia's portable

I also recommend using your string to practise knot untying whenever you can. Don't enter any of the less witch-friendly villages or towns until you can untie even the trickiest knots underwater.
– Miss Tick

Stones with holes in are known as 'hagstones'

'snail hotel' which is a quite luxurious, roomy and lettuce-lined purse.[1] I prefer to find my living elements on the fly and return them to their natural habitat with minimal discombobulation.

Some particularly useful iron implements

Iron

My first lesson on the importance of iron came when I smacked the monster Jenny Green-Teeth[2] in the face with my mother's biggest frying pan. It seemed a good idea at the time (a feeling I've since learned to curtail) since she was trying to snatch my brother, Wentworth, but it proved highly effective. I soon learned from Miss Tick that all otherworldly creatures detest iron. Although

I seem to recall you rather forced the encounter by using your brother as bait. – Miss Tick

1. Although unlikely to catch on as a must-have fashion item outside the witch world.

2. See Jenny Green-Teeth. Page 151

We was all very impressed. – E. Weatherwax

hitting most creatures in the face with a frying pan is pretty efficient most of the time too.

It's not clear why iron is so effective, although there are many theories. It is seen as a metal of man not of nature, and one that the fairies themselves cannot forge and so they fear it. Whatever the reason, it causes them great pain, and I've seen the most powerful of elves shrink away from it with absolute fear, which is more than enough to recommend it. Even just carrying an iron nail will suffice if you get into a bind with something of the more supernatural persuasion. Or perhaps keep a small bag of swarf (iron shavings) on you. A horseshoe above the door is also traditional for most witches' abodes and considered lucky. Many prefer to hang it upwards to keep the luck contained within the house. Others prefer to hang it downwards so the luck is showered on any visitors. However you choose to use iron, make sure it's around you as much as possible and easy to grab. Frying pans will always remain my iron accessory of choice, because there are so few weapons that you can cook bacon and eggs in after using.

You ain't seen dancing until you've seen an elf with a pinch of swarf down his pants!
— Nanny Ogg

Any visitor to a witch's house should consider themselves lucky!
— E. Weatherax

Only in the sense that they need all the luck they can get!

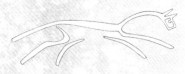

Lily Weatherwax, fairy godmother

Wands

While I didn't expect to be issued with a wand on day one, I was under the impression that they were a big part of being a witch. As it turns out, they aren't at all necessary. To my knowledge, the only witches to use them are those who think having impressive-looking tools makes them better at magiK. Any dealer in magical accoutrements will have a fancy array of wands on display. Most will be made of metal or rare woods carved with mystic runes and dotted with semi-precious stones and crystals. As impressive

as they look, bear in mind that there is nothing magical about wands. Just like wizards' staffs, they are a non-magical conduit for magic. Magic can actually be stored in them, but putting too much of yourself or your magic into an object is not a good idea.

If you must have a wand, just for the look of the thing, be sure to get the runes translated first. There's many a witch loftily waving wands inscribed with 'Oh What A Wally Is Waving This'. If you want a much cheaper option without embarrassing runes, see the 'Making Do' section later in this chapter.

Fairy godmothers' wands are a little different in that they really do hold magic of their own. Queen Magrat told me that she spent a short time as a fairy godmother and that mastering the wand was a lot trickier than just waving it and wishing hard. Her's was a long, slim, white rod with gold and silver rings along the length of it. She discovered that they could be twisted into different positions, allowing for different types of magic and transformation. Before you get too excited, this sort of wand is extremely rare. They are passed down from fairy godmother to fairy godmother and not available to buy anywhere. No one knows how many still exist, if any, especially as Magrat threw the last known one into the waters of the Vieux River in Genua.

That's right. I've seen wizards' staffs develop minds of their own after generations of magic being pumped through them. That's why I don't hold with wands. Tools can take as well as give.
– E. Weatherwax

At least we were never short of food on that trip. Well, pumpkins anyway!
– Nanny Ogg

She discovered? Surprised she didn't end up a pumpkin herself instead of queening it up down in Lancre!

A classic cauldron
- not typically used
for magic

Cauldrons

There's barely a week goes by without some small child asking me if I ever boil frogs, newts, eyeballs or even children in my cauldron. They're always disappointed when I tell them I don't even own one, and that my saucepan is barely big enough to fit a small cabbage into, never mind a child's head. A lot of witches do have cauldrons, typically inherited with their cottages, but they're a lot smaller than the illustrator of *The Goode Childe's Booke of Faerie Tales* would have you believe, and are only really used for stews, jams or boiling strips of cloth for bandages. Medicines and potions are more likely to be made by distillation or infusion, or the simple addition of sugar and berry juice to a bottle of water.[3]

Cauldrons are actually very important to Nac Mac Feegle keldas, and I was very interested to learn about Feegle cauldrons from Jeannie of the Chalk Hill clan. When a female Feegle leaves home to become kelda to another clan, she is gifted with a cauldron kit in the form of a triangle of tanned sheepskin wrapped around three wooden stakes, a string made of nettle fibres, and a hammer. This is the most ancient type of cauldron, from before humans ever started to work metals. The leather is tied to the three stakes pegged around a smouldering fire. Water is poured into it and the liquid slowly seeps into the leather, stopping the cauldron from burning as the water boils. Unlike the iron cauldrons of most witches, keldas don't use theirs for cooking but for true Feegle magic – accessing the memories of all the former clan matriarchs in their line.[4] Serius hiddlins! – Rob

If people from your steading regularly come to your home for help, you might find that they expect a very witchy cottage with a good old-fashioned cauldron large enough to boil a sheep. In this case, there's nothing wrong with employing a bit of boffo to meet their expectations.

3. *For those cases that simply require a dose of headology.*
4. *See* The Kelda. *Page 125*

Granny's gooseberry jam, good on toast, ideal for light masonry work

Gooseberry Jam

Boffo for the Home

While witches typically keep their cottages very clean, I've known several who made their homes look far more spooky with the wide range of exceptional and highly affordable items available from the Boffo Novelty and Joke Emporium's award-winning mail-order catalogue. _I feel dirty_ but this book needs sponsored advertising. More information from Mrs Proust below.

Don't worry Tiff, I feel dirty all the time. Never did me any harm!

— Nanny Ogg

Special Sheep Liniment

This is my father's name for what Granny Aching used to brew in the old cowshed. I wasn't meant to know about it, but the Feegles certainly did and view it as some kind of sacred elixir. It was undoubtedly some kind of moonshine, but any food or beverage created by a witch has a touch of magic about it. After the creation of Horace[5] I know that only too well. My father used to swear it was the best nightcap going and Feegles will do just about anything for a drop of the stuff, which makes it a useful tool for both protection and persuasion. There's very little of it left now and my father has not been able to replicate it.

Addendum: I found part of the Special Sheep Liniment recipe tucked into the spine of *Diseases of the Sheep*[6] which was passed down to me after Granny Aching's death. I've been trying to recreate the recipe myself in the hope that it can become a useful witching tool in small quantities. The Feegles have proved to be very enthusiastic taste-testers, but i no longer conduct the tests in the shepherd's hut after Daft Wullie took half the roof off. So far it does not yet dissolve spoons, but it does tarnish them so i think i'm on the right track.

5. *See* Horace, the Honorary Feegle. *Page 128*
6. *The nearest thing Granny Aching had to a journal.*

He canne walk in a str8 line yet, but he wasne gud at tha to start wif!
— Rob

Making Do

As I said at the start of this chapter, all a witch really needs is her hat. For everything else the best of us make do. Mistress Weatherwax once told me, 'Get your mind right and you can make a stick your wand.' She was right; just thinking of items in the right way can make them fit for purpose. You can scry in a saucer of ink, shoot flames from a stick, even make a frying pan your magic sword. When it comes down to tools, witches can manage the same tasks as wizards with much less of a show and specialist equipment. Most of us are aware that the elaborate incantations and equipment required in most rites can be simplified down to the most basic items representing the intended equipment. You just have to mean the words and imagine the items to be real. Witches make do because we know that the real power lies inside of us, not in our tools.

Exactly! Did we ever tell you about the time we summoned the demon Wxrttbtl-jwlpklz in my washtub with old soap flakes, a scrubbing brush and a copper stick? I still think of him every time I rinse out my unmentionables.

— Nanny Ogg

They hardly seems unmentionable, you brings them up all the time.

— E. Weatherwax

Flint – the bones of the chalk

THE POWER OF THE LAND

As witches, we draw our magic from the earth. It might not be sentient in quite the same way as us, but that doesn't mean it isn't alive. The land was born millions of years before us, and will be here for millions more after it takes us back into its arms. Witches work in harmony with the earth. We grow the herbs we need for medicines, keep animals to provide honey, eggs and dairy, and to turn our kitchen scraps to manure. We weave our own baskets, even our caskets, from willow branches. We reuse and recycle, and trade anything we have too much of for other things that we need. The land is ours and we belong to the land. We look after each other and draw power from each other, but the relationship between magic and earth is greater than that. There is more a witch should know about the magic of the land and how it can rise up and lend its strength to those most in tune with it in their hour of need.

Some witches believe very strongly in the effect of local geology on magic. I've asked Miss Tick to write about this as it is a subject of great interest to her.

In relation to Miss Tick's thoughts on geology, I once asked Mrs Proust[1] how she could be a witch in Ankh-Morpork, a city built on slime and mud. She told me that cities are built from granite and marble and chert – everywhere you look, stone and rock. Every cobble has once had blood on it and a witch can reach down with her bones, feel the living stones and listen to their story – the rock that built city upon city buoying you up against the tug of the world and lending you its power.

A witch's bones can tell you an awful lot. My left elbow is surprisingly informative.
– Miss Tick

1. *See* Enterprising Witches. *Page 33*

Geology and Witchcraft
Miss Perspicacia Tick

Being particularly sensitive to geology myself, I'm always aware of the composition of the land I travel through. Research and past experience have taught me that solid rock, good granite or basalt are the best foundations for those with magical tendencies to thrive. This is why so many of the finest witches and wizards on the Disc hail from the Ramtops. I've always been wary of chalk country, as that's where I feel at my weakest. The Chalk wasn't somewhere I ventured as a witchfinder as I always said that chalk is too soft to grow a witch on. Honest soil, and even clay, is fine, but chalk is soggy and damp – it's neither one thing nor the other. However, Tiffany Aching turned all I thought I knew on its head.

What I failed to consider was the nature of chalklands. The Chalk was once alive, in the form of billions of sea creatures that finally became the land itself. Tiffany draws on the strength of the Chalk, its life energy, its memories and the hardness at its heart. As Mistress Weatherwax pointed out to me, 'The bones of the hills is flint. It's hard and sharp and useful'. Words that could equally describe the fine witch grown on those hills. Perhaps whatever the land we stand upon, there is always a strength to be found if we know how to reach for it.

Calkins – known as Chalk children on the downs

A relic from when the Chalk was a vast ocean

Land Memories

The strength of the land lies in its memories. The mountains remember when they were created from molten rock or a colossal clashing of the Disc's plates. Deserts remember when they were prehistoric savannahs. When I first fought the queen of Fairyland I was nearly beaten on my own turf. But as I lay there with the cold and darkness closing in, the land reached up and drew me down into its memories. Within its embrace I saw the birth of the Chalk. The land under wave.[2] The shells of billions of creatures that became the land itself. The land lent me something. I felt as tall as the sky, as old as the hills, as strong as the sea. The price of that, and the reward,[3] was that I had to give it back. The land chooses us. Witches are born to protect its borders. We have to fight for it, to speak for that which has no voice, only memories.

2. *Interestingly this translates as 'Tir-farthóinn' in Feegle-tongue.*

3. *To be that awake and see it all as it really is… no human could stand that for long.*

Aye, the Chalk nose the hiddlins as wel as any Kelda.
— Rob

A distinctive area of gnarly ground

Gnarly Ground

There are places where the magic of the land can work against us. Gnarly country – large expanses of magical land that were compressed as continents crashed together and gave birth to mountains. This is another reason why there's so much magic in the Ramtops, and why so many witches and powerful wizards are born there.

Witches are particularly susceptible to the effects of gnarly ground. The way you feel affects how you experience it. If you're happy, it's a beautiful moor in bloom with babbling brooks. If you're <u>angry or afraid</u>, it's full of thorns and deep ravines with raging rivers. As I mentioned in a previous chapter, it's hard to scry into gnarly ground because the magic swirling around it causes <u>interference</u>. It's risky to try to perform magic in a place like that, which even interferes with the flight of broomsticks far above it.

Confidence helps too. Agnes Nitt almost fell into a ravine on gnarly ground, but that other personality of hers – the cocky one – took over. The raging river a mile below was a short drop into a little stream for Ms Perdita X Dream.
— Nanny Ogg

All reasons why it's a good place to hide yourself away, to be alone with your thoughts or to develop your plans of attack, should you ever need to.
— E. Weatherwax

The Dancers

Stone Circles and Doorways

You've probably seen lots of stone circles in both the Ramtops and the Chalk, often built from rock quarried many miles away. The travelling teachers told me that most were built by druids, to function as calendars, but there are also the Other Ones – stone circles like The Dancers in the overgrown moorland of Lancre, and the three trilithon markers up on the downlands of the Chalk. They aren't just decoration. They're there for the land's protection. They mark thin areas between worlds, making it easier for guardians to look to these doorways for any sign of trouble. There are many thin areas that haven't been found and marked yet – some come and go as other worlds briefly press against ours, others are always there as they latch on like ticks.

They may be called The Dancers, but they should NEVER be danced around. You don't want to draw the attention of them what live in the world beyond!

– E. Weatherwax

The presence of a strong witch[4] protects the land, making it harder for anything to pass through these thin places. But when the strongest among us pass away it causes ripples across the land and a weakening of the borders. At those times we must be especially careful to look to the edges.

As Nanny Ogg tells it, The Dancers were dragged together to encircle a thin area and to make sure nothing ever passed through that breach. They aren't even stone, they're a sort of thunderbolt iron that fell from the sky. It draws metal to it and is the one thing elves can't bear over iron itself. Petulia and I tried flying over them once, just to see what happened. It's impossible. It's like an invisible wall extending up beyond our atmosphere, caging in the entrance to Fairyland, the home of the elves. Now that the railways are expanding across the Disc the land is bound in iron and a lot less enticing for elves. But their parasitic world is still there, and the elves wait for a time when even the iron in our heads rusts.

Hill Carvings and Symbols

There are many barrows that dot the land. These aren't just burial mounds. Some are home to Feegle clans, who assume that the dead kings won't mind sharing their space as well as their gold. There are also more surprisingly shaped earthworks, such as the Long Man barrow in Lancre which consists of two circular domes and a long one. Lucy Warbeck insists on flying every new witch in

4. See Edge Witches. *Page 40*

I mite be the big man, but hes the big-big man! - Rob

And how would Gytha Ogg know that, J wonders?
- E. Weatherwax

Practically a rite of passage for Ogg women to take their daughters up there to watch the show over their first drop of scumble.

Want to know the tree with the best view?
— Nanny Ogg

training over it when they first get a broomstick. It's over six years since she started flying and she *still* giggles so much she can barely fly straight! As clearly symbolized, this is a male space. As Nanny Ogg <u>tells it</u>, men gather here by moonlight, naked but for horns, to drink and wrestle and dance around open fires – in much the same manner as the creatures deep below. Down there, beneath the Long Man, is another trilithon made of the same iron as The Dancers. It frames another gateway to another elven land, but that one belongs to the King, whose nature is clear by his <u>mark on the land</u>.

No one remembers who created the chalk carvings, why they are there, or who they were for – just that they are important. They're scattered over the hills, deep white scars in the earth in the shapes of animals and well-endowed giants. The people of the Chalk are proud of the carvings and tend to them, keeping

Near enough a scale model it is too!
— Nanny Ogg

About as much as J wants a porcupine in my privy!

them alive. Shepherds weed them to keep them clear when they're passing with their flocks and, during the annual scouring fair, everyone is expected to bring a small shovel or knife to grub up the weeds and make the carvings stand out boldly. There's always a lot of giggling from the girls working on the giant.

The White Horse of the Chalk might not look like a horse if you don't know horses. It's not meant to. It's more the essence of a horse captured in motion. When a hiver attacked at the Lancre Witch Trials, the spirit of the White Horse rose up and galloped into the mountains to lend me its strength. Perhaps that's what the carvings really are – protectors of the land and those who serve it, and symbols to remind us where we're from and to <u>where we will return</u>.

Though sometimes, just sometimes, they're the land's way of shouting 'I've got a great big tonker!'

MRS LETICE EARWIG
HIGHER MAGIK, PROFESSIONAL SPELLS

While understanding the power of the land is indeed important to every witch, it appears that in her youth, Miss Aching has failed to consider the power of what lies above. A witch should understand the messages written in the stars and the power of lunar and solar magic. The fact that we stand on the Disc should not stop us from looking beyond her skies. See my book The Higher MagiK for a detailed exploration of the power of the celestial bodies.

FAMILIARS & COMPANIONS

No matter how often you go around the houses, or how many covens you join, sometimes being a witch can be rather lonely. When you've been out in all weathers sewing up wounds, dispensing justice or cleaning an old man's false teeth, you need something to come home to. Whilst many witches never find a partner, or even desire to, it can be a comfort to have a little bit of company. That's when many turn to familiars – sentient creatures who live their lives beside their witch and not only provide company but also useful skills and, depending on the chosen familiar, a good deal of boffo[1] to boot.

Some of those you meet along your personal path to witch-hood will be a little more talkative, and perhaps more challenging, than your average familiar. These may suit those who prefer a less solitary home-life, or value having someone to talk to while on the move. Some you'll gravitate to, others will gravitate to you (whether you'd like them to or not) and most will have been touched by magic in some way.

1. See Boffo. Page 64

A gift from you to me

Greebo

Aw, look at Mummy's
handsome boy!
I'd be very obliged if
Mister Kidby could
send me a framed copy
to put on the dresser
next to our Shirl
—Nanny Ogg

Dinnae fash yersel
-pussy kat! — Rob

Cats

Felines are the traditional familiar of choice for a witch. Whether
they are magically inclined themselves or just drawn to magic, cats
and witches often go together like a cup of tea and a biscuit. That
is aside from Mistress Weatherwax. Cats go together with her like
Special Sheep Liniment and spoons.

Having shared lodgings with Nanny Ogg on a number of occasions, I have often been around her infamous cat, Greebo. Beloved by Nanny and the scourge of Lancre's wildlife (up to and including wolves and bears), Greebo is best described as underbridled rage in a cat costume. Greebo is most definitely an Ogg, given the number of his offspring in Lancre and his tendency to gravitate towards a warm spot. Possibly a fiend from hell, he has unstable morphology due to a spell placed on him by Nanny, Magrat and Mistress Weatherwax whereupon he became temporarily human. Or, at least somewhere between a cat-like human and a human-like cat. I've never seen this myself, but Nanny says it left a 'lasting impression' on a number of ladies in the vicinity.

Given that he has killed or maimed both vampires and elves, I was surprised to learn that there are some things that even Greebo fears. He certainly gives a wide berth to the Feegles. Although a certain amount of giving a wide berth to Feegles is a sensible idea for most creatures. But chief amongst his few fears, the one that gets him cowering behind the pot shelf, is You[2] – the white cat I gave, as a kitten, to Mistress Weatherwax.

Given her general dislike of cats, this was a risky move. But there was something about this little ball of white fur. Something in the way she held herself. No bigger than a potato, she had the self-assurance of a mountain range. It was almost

He's a big softy really.
— Nanny Ogg

Takes after his mummy he does
—Nanny Ogg

2. *A contraction of 'Stop that, You!'*

Weatherwaxian. On top of that, You's mother, Pinky, was one of a number of cats who belonged to the Widow Cable. When the old lady passed away, it was over two months before her body was discovered. The cats, along with a litter of pure white kittens that were born on the old lady's bed, had prioritized survival over sentimentality. I had terrible difficulty finding homes for them until, at least for You, I found someone with equally practical priorities.

You

Addendum: Since the death of Mistress Weatherwax, You has come to live with me. She's taken well to the shepherd's hut and on occasion I have seen her riding around on the backs of the local sheep, as if they were ambulatory beds. She is as self-assured as ever and occasionally looks at me with a stare that somehow seems... familiar.

Thunder

Lightning

Dogs

If you're not really a cat person, you may be surprised to learn that dogs can be excellent companions for a witch. Whilst the independent nature of cats fits well with the average witch's lifestyle, dogs are less self-reliant and therefore tend to be less popular. That being said, dogs can be of far more practical help to witches. The presence of canine companions was an innate part of my early childhood, in the form of Thunder and Lightning, Granny Aching's black and white sheepdogs.

Wherever she went they were right by her side, apart from the times when they were rounding up the sheep, which they did better than any creature on the Chalk – man or beast. They always seemed to know what Granny wanted them to do. She barely had to utter a command. I remember the times when I used to run around the lowlands trying my hand at ordering them to round up the sheep. I'd shout, 'Come by!' and 'Away to me' and they'd obey. I was so proud I walked on air. Granny just watched, puffing away on her old pipe and occasionally nodding approvingly. Later I realized that they knew what they were doing without a single command needed.

When Granny died, the dogs waited until she was buried then trotted away across the turf. Whilst they disappeared from the Chalk that day, and possibly this realm, they have come to my aid on the occasions where it felt right to call on them. I was never certain if I was calling on creatures of spirit, flesh or just manifestations of the Chalk itself, but whatever those incarnations were, they proved to be formidable foes against both nightmarish creatures from Fairyland and the elves themselves. I felt Granny's presence running through them and it gave me the strength to face things I never thought I could.

Goats

Mephistopheles

Most of the older witches, especially those who live on their own, keep goats. This is one animal where the line between familiar and livestock blurs a little. For someone who is used to sheep, I found goats a little harder to relate to. A goat is like a sheep, but with a brain, which means you have to use your own brain to deal with them. They will try every trick to mess you about – a favourite being placing a hoof straight into the middle of a full milk pail. Or, if they're feeling particularly malevolent (which is most of the time), kicking it right across the milking yard.

Even when dealing with a small herd of goats, there is a hierarchy involved. Like witches, they have somewhat of a pecking order. The trick is to establish yourself as head-goat.

Never slap them, no matter how much they provoke you. It's like hitting a sack full of coat hangers and you're most likely to hurt yourself – then the goat will have won. And, again like witches, to a goat winning is *everything*.

When dealing with the goat that thinks it is the <u>head-goat,</u> never neglect the power of embarrassment. With Black Meg, Miss Level's senior nanny, I learnt that grabbing her leg as she raised it to kick, and lifting it just a little higher, unbalanced her and made her nervous. This made her look silly in front of the other goats who sniggered at her. I won.

Once you establish yourself as head-goat you'll find that goats can make very useful additions to a witch's steading. They produce nutritious milk, which can be used in various remedies, and they will eat almost anything. They provide protection too; a well-trained billy goat can guard as well as any dog, and I once saw Black Meg stamp an adder to death.

Geoffrey Swivel's[3] goat, Mephistopheles, is one of the most intelligent familiars I've ever come across, despite being one of the smelliest. The runt of the litter, he was raised by Geoffrey from a kid and has stayed by his side ever since. He has a mind of his own, if not several minds, and it feels like there's a definite purpose to his presence here that may become clear in time. He is able to count, use the privy and round up sheep. Due to his neat and twinkly little hooves, and the fact that she once saw him sitting in the middle of a circle of wild goats, Nanny nicknamed him the Mince of Darkness. But Mephistopheles' hooves are not to be underestimated, neither are his horns and teeth, as the elf Lord Lankin found out when he tried to go head-to-horn with him.

3. *See* Geoffrey Swivel. *Page 184*

For lower goats, an ear nip will establish dominance. This doesn't hurt, because it's like biting a carpet, but it surprises them enough for you to get on with the task of milking.
– Miss Tick

That reminds me of the late Mr Ogg – he ~~was very~~ ~~~~
– Nanny Ogg

Birds

Miss Treason was partial to avian familiars who also doubled as her eyes after she went blind. When I first joined her she had a jackdaw, which was later replaced by a mouse. The mouse was particularly disconcerting as she would hold it out on her palm in front of her, swinging it around to face you when she spoke. The pink wriggly nose was rather creepy and I was relieved when she replaced it with two ravens. Ravens also add a lot of natural boffo to proceedings. Certainly a lot more than Lightfoot, the tortoise Queen Magrat once had as a familiar. I saw one at a fair once and it looked as though it wouldn't strike fear into anything except lettuce.

Nanny tells me that Mrs Gogol had as her familiar 'The biggest cock I've ever seen. And I've seen a few in my time' – a creature named Legba who was either a dark and dangerous spirit, or just a big, black cockerel. It crowed mainly at sunset and had the same effect on alligators that Greebo had on wolves and bears, but Nanny's cat (who accompanied her to Genua) did not warm to Legba. Possibly he didn't like the competition.

What with me living next to a chicken farm and all!
— Nanny Ogg

Miss Eumenides
Treason with her
avian familiars

Bees

Like goats, bees fulfil a handy role in a steading – producing honey, wax and royal jelly, which can be very handy when making a poultice for a wound, baking and making particularly good dribbly candles. A beehive is a marvellous thing to behold and it's no surprise that I have encountered several beekeeping witches. Mistress Weatherwax was the first, and she learned much about the art of beekeeping from Mr Brooks, the former Royal Beekeeper of Lancre castle.[4] Her hives were always busy and humming, no matter what the time of year. Although she was immensely skilled in borrowing,[5] it took many years before she could borrow the mind, or minds, of an <u>entire hive</u>.

She swanked about that for weeks.
— Nanny Ogg

Miss Level was also an accomplished beekeeper and would spend a great deal of time <u>talking to her bees</u>. And whilst Mistress Weatherwax would sometimes do the same, she taught me that it was more important to listen to them. Bees see and hear everything. There is no doubt that bees are intelligent and knowledgeable, but they also have a sense of… well, almost fun too.

It is tradition for keepers to tell their bees about important events. Many even share little bits of news and gossip. It is said that failure to inform the bees of their keeper's death will result in them leaving the hive or failing to produce honey. — Miss Tick

Mistress Weatherwax's bees once formed into the shape of a witch right in front of me! I danced with her in the glowing light; a thousand beating wings and jewelled eyes whirling along with my steps. It's moments like these, the golden moments, which make it all worthwhile. They will see you through even the darkest of times.

4. See Almost Witches. *Page 180*

5. See Borrowing. *Page 68*

Toad

Amphibians

Given the popularity of turning people into toads, frogs or the occasional newt, within certain fringe elements of witch society, I have made it a rule to always attempt to converse with amphibians on sight, just in case they have recently experienced an unstable morphology and might be in need of aid. Or, failing that, a fat slug.

The first talking amphibian I encountered was a toad.[6] He was, by his own admission, not familiar, just slightly presumptuous, and believed himself to be a human who had been turned into a toad. However, he once confided in me that

---

6. *Who wants to make it very clear that he should, in no way, be considered a humorous talking animal.*

Don't try kissing them, even if you are a princess. You're more likely to end up with a face full of slime than uncover a cursed prince.
– Miss Tick

Young Gytha learnt this the hard way!

Thank you Mrs Ogg. Toads need love too

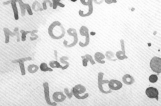

he used to wake in the middle of the night – the ghosts of a thousand bluebottles buzzing in his ears – and wonder if he was ever really human. Perhaps he was always just a toad who was made to think that he was once human.

Toad did eventually recollect that he was once a lawyer named Mr James Natter, who was employed to sue a fairy godmother of some renown for failing to properly fulfil the three wishes she'd bestowed upon a local princess. The result of the case was that the princess ended up as a hand-mirror[7] and her lawyer ended up with an insatiable desire to eat flies and skulk in ponds.

Although the Feegles' weapons normally glow blue in the presence of lawyers, this doesn't appear to be true for lawyers with an amphibian wrapping. A relief for Toad who now lives with the Chalk Hill Feegles as their pro-bono lawyer. He says the Feegle life suits him and he has a plentiful supply of snails. It's also fairly peaceful as very few legal cases are ever brought against the Feegles. And if there are, then they are brought to a conclusion quite quickly, usually with a good kickin'.

Human brains are like clay. Easily shaped. Some deserve it, but personally I don't hold with messin' with animals' minds.
– E. Weatherwax

Unless it's Greebo?
– Nanny Ogg

We ALL did that. Besides, he's less animal, more demon.

The Feegle-legal way!
– Rob

7. *Making her much more useful than most princesses.*

The late Baron
Saturday

Mrs Gogol

The Undead

Dabbling in the affairs of life and death is all part and parcel of
being a witch, although ideally there'll be more of the former
than the latter. There may be times when you are called to bring
others back from the brink of death, and even beyond.[8] But once
you get much further you get into necromancy territory, which is
something I hope never to have the need to dabble in.

Nanny Ogg told me that during their adventures in Genua
they discovered that Mrs Gogol had her own zombie consort,
named Baron Saturday – the late, but still very present, father of
Ella Saturday, the young girl Magrat had suddenly become
godmother to. Nanny, who generally adjusts quickly to almost
every scenario, was surprised to see that Mistress Weatherwax
barely blinked at the presence of a dead man serving her <u>stew</u>.

8. See Life & Death. Page 190

*I'll admit that I did look quite
closely at the lady's fingers in it.
Well you never know.*
— Nanny Ogg

A hole chapta? Wait til I tells the lads wes famouse!
– ROb

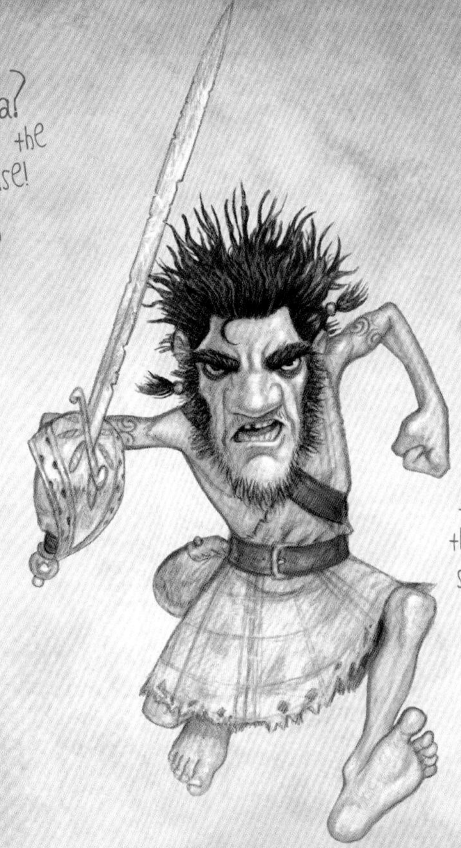

Rob Anybody

Is mutch betta lookin than tha! Mista Kidby, ya scunner! Yes headin fer a kickin!

THE NAC MAC FEEGLE

Ah yes, the Nac Mac Feegle, the Wee Free Men or alternatively 'Person or Persons Unknown, Believed to Be Armed'. I'm sure you'll be wanting to know *all* about them. Forewarned is forearmed, so they say, but I suggest that any arming you do against the Feegles includes your fastest boots and a bottle of Special Sheep Liniment to throw in your wake.

Might I also suggest the Feegle chapter and glossary in my very own book Fairies and How to Avoid Them as further reading on this subject.
– Miss Tick

Crakin' plan! No notes!

Pictsies

If you're anything like me and grew up under the influence of *The Goode Childe's Booke of Faerie Tales*, then you might have been fooled into believing that pixies (or pictsies as the Feegle are known) are cute and mischievous, relatively harmless creatures who might be persuaded to help out with the household chores in exchange for a saucer of milk. Do not, *under any circumstances*, attempt this. If you're lucky, you'll be picking bits of saucer out of the furniture. If you're unlucky, you'll be picking the furniture out of you. That being said, most Feegles tend to have an innate respect for <u>witches</u>, so you might just get away with being drenched in milk amidst various mutterings of '<u>Mudlin, hag</u>! D'ya think wez a bunch o' <u>bunties</u>?' And believe me, you'll have got off lightly.

Y'dunae cross a pointy bonnet!
— Rob

A useless person.

A witch of any age. More respectful than it might seem.
— Miss Tick

A weak person. A terrible insult to a Feegle.

Big Yan

Medium Sized Jock (with traditional helmet)

Know Your Feegle

Feegles are typically known for three things: stealin', drinkin' and fightin'. Preferably all three at the same time if <u>they can get away with it</u>. And they often do get away with it due to their immense speed and strength. However, running out of enemies is never an issue as Feegles are quite content to go on fighting amongst themselves once all available foes have been dispatched.

An' we often does!

Feegles have a distinct appearance, with wild red hair and blue skin – or so it appears from a distance. Those who have survived meeting one up close will know that the blue is actually a swirling mass of clan tattoos and woad. Due to the headbutt being their preferred form of attack, their noses are likely to be as skewed as their views on property ownership. The only item of clothing worn by a Feegle is a kilt, over which they hang their spog – a small pouch, which you'll often see them scratching as there's a good chance the contents are still alive and wriggling. And possibly being used as a handkerchief or intended as a future snack.

Accessories typically include feathers and beads in their hair and beards, helmets made of rodent skulls and weapons fashioned from whatever they can scavenge, including old men's toenails. This speaks to the Feegles' natural resourcefulness, which I've always been impressed by, even when it's caused me a certain amount of inconvenience. I once caught Hamish, the clan's buzzard-riding scout, using my second-best bloomers as a makeshift parachute to aid in a safer descent to the ground. So keep in mind that if your undergarments start going missing, you might just have a Feegle about.

These make particularly lethal daggers.
– Miss Tick

Hard as flint!
– Rob

As the Feegles sent to pose for Mister Kidby spent most of their time whizzing around his studio seeking out bottles of turps, he gave up painting their individual woad tattoos, and instead depicted them as entirely blue. If you find yourself in a position where you might see a Feegle's tattoos up close in the wild, then you are likely beyond any help this book could provide. – Ronald Goatberger

WANTED
Crivens!

Report all sightings to Chief Constable
Upshot of the Shires Watch

Rob Anybody

Daft Wullie

Awfully Wee Billy Bigchin

Big Yan

A handy guide
to identifying
members of the
Chalk Hill Feegle
clan

Hamish

Wee Dangerous Spike

Fion

Wee Jock Jock

William the Gonnagle

No-As-Big-As-Medium-Jock-But-
Bigger-Than-Wee-Jock-Jock

Etchings kindly provided by Master Kidby of the Engraver's Guild

Ooh, yes is a grass
noo then Mista Kidby! —
Rob

Feegle History

The history of the Feegles goes back almost as far as history itself. Since the first tetrapod shuffled out of the mud and shouted 'Crivens!' before headbutting the nearest rock. Whilst they fall under an extremely broad definition of 'fairy folk', it's not clear whether they originated in Fairyland[1] or simply wandered into it one day on the off chance of a fight. Either way, their time serving Queen Nightshade, the former ruler of Fairyland, ended with their exile. Perhaps, as many of them claim, it was due to their own rebellion against her cruel rule. But more likely, they just got booted out for being drunk and extremely disorderly. Whatever led to it also led to the Feegles' motto and favoured battle cry: 'Nae king! Nae quin! Nae laird! Nae master! We willnae' be fooled again!'

Whether rebels or exiles, the Feegles were invaluable in helping me gain access to Fairyland and take on Queen Nightshade herself after she stole my brother Wentworth, when he was little more than a ball of stickiness and a big grin. Although the Feegles generously let me discover the way into Fairyland for myself, by finding a place where time didn't fit,[2] they have the innate ability to freely cross into other worlds, dimensions and even dreams. This is via a manoeuvre known as the crawstep. If you were watching the

A general exclamation which can mean anything from 'I'm very surprised!' to 'Stand back, something is about to regret being alive!'

– Miss Tick

1. *A parasitic world that latches on to and feeds off other worlds. Rather like a sheep-tick.*

2. *See Stone Circles and Doorways. Page 98*

Feegle history resists limiting itself to just facts

process, you'd see a Feegle stick one leg out in front of them, wiggle their foot, and disappear as they shift between dimensions.

Most Feegles don't think too much about where they come from or where they are going to. They very much exist in the present. They like this world. In fact, they consider it so marvellous and full of things to drink, fight and eat, that they have reasoned that it must be some kind of reward for them, and therefore they are clearly dead. When a Feegle dies, as we think of it, it's considered like being born anew. They'll go off to the next world and if they are good Feegles there, they will be rewarded by returning to our world. It goes to show that what may seem ordinary and unremarkable to you can be heaven to someone else.

Bigjobs din nae how gud yez got it! —Rob

It may seem from my words that Feegles are <u>dangerous, drunken</u> louts who should be avoided at all costs. And that is very true. However, I have also found them to be smart (individually rather than collectively), brave and fiercely loyal to those they have sworn to protect. They care deeply for their clan and have a sense of family and community spirit that puts most humans to shame.

Tis fair!

They are also willing to evolve, especially if it teaches them more about the world they love so much. When I first met the Chalk Hill Feegle clan, they were <u>deeply suspicious of reading</u> and writing, and viewed the act of writing things down to be as potent as any spell.

A sentiment I happen to share.
- E. Weatherwax

Whilst the right words at the right time can move mountains, their attitude towards the written word has softened a lot over the years thanks to their new kelda, Jeannie, who encouraged her new Feegle family to embrace the pen as mightily as the sword or old man's toenail. This had already been adopted for many years by Big Aggie, Jeannie's mother and kelda of the Long Lake clan.

Although the Chalk Hill Feegles have a way to go in this regard, most of what they write is approaching legible, and they've stopped wailing and chewing their spogs in fear whenever they hear the unscrewing of an inkpot lid. Much of this has been aided by Toad, who showed them that the legal words and doings they had feared for so long could also be used to their benefit. Once the Feegles see something as a weapon, they feel a lot more relaxed about it.

Wes all miss ye, Ma! — Rob

Maeve

The Kelda

Before I was a witch, I was a kelda. Although I always thought of myself as a temporary kelda, put in place by Maeve, the old Chalk Hill clan's kelda, just before her death, until another could be found. Since this meant that at nine years of age I suddenly gained a fiancé who only came up to the top of my boots,[3] it was clearly never going to last.

As a result of this position and my subsequent friendship with Jeannie, who eventually (and thankfully) replaced me, I had to learn a lot about the art of keldaring. And since a kelda is the

---

3. *Rob Anybody, the head of the Chalk Hill clan's warriors, who looked more terrified at the prospect than I did.*

nearest Feegles come to having a witch of their own, it's important that you know too.

A Feegle mound (Feegles prefer living underground) can be considered rather like a beehive, if the only reason bees left was to get drunk, pick fights and return with stolen goods rather than pollen. The kelda is like the queen bee; she rules over the clan as its leader and mother to most of it. A kelda will have hundreds of male offspring, but female babies are very rare, with a kelda only having one or two during her lifetime. Unlike a hive, a daughter cannot take over her mother's clan and must one day leave with some of her brothers to find a clan without a kelda and select a husband, who will henceforth be known as the 'Big Man' to lead the warriors. If there is no clan without a kelda, she may form one of her own, choose a husband, and make a home in the nearest available ancient burial mound, cave system or empty rabbit warren.

Almost all rabbit warrens are empty when Feegles live nearby. Or soon will be.
— Miss Tick

Tasty conies!

Like witches, keldas are strong-willed and magically inclined. They are extremely adept at a type of healing known as the 'soothings', which heals the mind as well as the body and even induces sleep. Something I was very glad of when my mind was too cluttered and noisy to welcome sleep in the normal way.

Keldas also have knowledge of the 'hiddlins' – all the Feegle secrets. These are ancient and closely guarded and, outside of the kelda–daughter bond, only shared with those they feel a strong kinship with.[4] When a Feegle daughter leaves her clan to make her way in the world as a fully-fledged kelda, she takes a flask of her mother's cauldron water with her. Just one drop of it added to her own cauldron water allows her to tap into the wisdom of all the keldas who have come before her. One drink and she is immersed in a sea of memories. Jeannie tells me that this helps to ease the pain of leaving her birth-clan. For a kelda can never return home. They are home.

Alongside guiding their own established clan, keldas often fulfil a similar role to that of an edge witch,[5] namely protecting our world from assault from other worlds. Before Maeve died, she told me that she had struck up quite a friendship with my Granny Aching over the years. On a cold night, these two edge protectors would often share a smoke, or a drop or two of Special Sheep Liniment,[6] whilst huddled around Granny's pot-bellied stove in the heart of her shepherd's hut. Though much time has passed since then, it's a mental image that still warms me as much as that stove.

Jeannie and two offspring

4. See Part-time Witches. *Page 175*
5. See Edge Witches. *Page 40*
6. See Special Sheep Liniment. *Page 91*

Horace
the cheese — the
first Cheegle

Horace, the Honorary Feegle

I always knew I was good with cheese, but I didn't know just
how good until I accidentally created Horace, while perfecting
my Lancre Blue recipe. All cheese is a little bit alive anyway, but
Horace is a lot alive. He moves around on his own, often at great
speed, and is a better mouse catcher than most cats. He has also
been known to eat other cheeses, which feels very wrong. He's
somehow more than a familiar, although his companionability is

questionable. He makes a soft snoring sound when asleep, which is surprisingly relaxing. I once caught him nudging my leg to show me all the mouse tails sticking out of his cheesy depths.

Like Toad, Horace has found his calling with the Feegles of the Chalk Hill clan. Perhaps his blue veins reminded them of their own numerous tattoos, but they embraced him as a rotund brother. He sports their tartan and even fights with them in battle; being particularly adept at 'elf bowling'. I even heard him trying to shout 'Crivens!' at one point but it just came out as 'MMmnnah!' Strangely, I still felt a twinge of pride. Nevertheless, let Horace be a warning to you to always keep your magic under control. You never know when some might leak out and into a nearby dairy product.

Horace is a fine Feegle an givs a nuttin that ud send a bear cross-eyed— Rob

A WITCH'S ABODE

Country witches usually live within their steadings, typically in a cottage that has been passed down from witch to witch over the decades. Whilst this is the traditional way of things, there's no rule stating that a witch must live in an ancient, thatched cottage out in the woods. Some live in modern homes at the heart of their steadings, others choose homes that can travel with them. Witch-wizard Eskarina Smith's cottage lies deep within a pile of magical waste outside the Unseen University walls. At the other end of the scale, Queen Magrat lives in a huge, rambling castle. Though she is no longer a full-time witch, the whole kingdom could now be considered her steading and she steps up to protect it whenever she is needed.

Thanks to the likes of *The Goode Childe's Booke of Faerie Tales*, people also think of witches' homes as dank, dirty hovels, but every witch's house I've been inside is spotless. Mostly because of the hard work of their apprentices, though in the case of Miss Level, her invisible ondageist, Oswald, cleans her cottage, whereas Mrs Ogg's cottage is kept clean by her daughters-in-law who are only invisible to Mrs Ogg. With witches inhabiting everything from traditional rustic cottages through to shepherd's huts, castles and pristine new builds, it's clear that all a house actually needs to become a true witch's cottage is a resident witch. Cat optional.

Anyone got a magnifying glass for these spill words?

— Nanny Ogg

The Traditional Cottage

The cottages passed from witch to witch over the decades have often been extended and mended to the extent that the oldest contain very little of the original materials they were built with. The walls bulge and corkscrew-chimneys poke through thatch so old that there are probably creatures presumed extinct living in it. It can be difficult to even work out what the original buildings looked like. Gardens are put to practical use. The half that isn't home to goats, beehives and chickens, is planted with vegetables and both cooking and medicinal herbs. Mistress Weatherwax's cottage, a mile or so outside the village of Bad Ass, ticks all of these boxes and her herb garden is a thing of legend, boasting an eerie collection of strange, hairy, spiky or grasping plants with odd flowers or weird seed pods.

The Herbs know me, but anyone else headin' in there had better take a stout stick, mebbe an axe, for defendin' themselves.

— E. Weatherwax

The Modern Cottage

Livin' in town is fine for them what don't mind constant visitors. Ain't no one walking a mile to the witch in the woods for just a scraped ankle.

— E. Weatherwax

One might argue (not me of course) that nobody would do that with a broken ankle either.

— Miss Tick

These days, a lot of young witches prefer more modern housing closer to town, which makes going around the houses and visiting the sick far easier. It's more the older witches who prefer the traditional, solitary dwellings. After living in Miss Treason's deliberately creepy old cottage, which was black from floor to rafters, I was very surprised by the difference when I moved into Nanny Ogg's newly built cottage right in the heart of Lancre's town square. But then, Mrs Ogg is always defying expectations.

Tir Nani Ogg has a perfect, freshly thatched roof and immaculate lawn with a tiny pond. The only toadstools are brightly painted ornaments, alongside pink bunnies and big-eyed deer. There isn't even a Boffo cobweb or skull in sight as the shelves are filled with jolly ornaments from her legion of

Proud to say I've never met an expectation I couldn't defy!

— Nanny Ogg

You forgot the gnome widdling in the pond.

— Nanny Ogg

No one forgets the gnome widdlin' in the pond.

children and grandchildren. Nanny's cottage doesn't advertize that she's a witch, but when you're a witch with as much respect and experience as her, I guess you don't have to.

If you like to advertize, it is possible to show that even a grand manor house belongs to a witch if you decorate it the right way. Mrs Earwig's home has expensive magical items everywhere, from a silver five-pointed star on the door, expensive curse-nets, huge witchy pictures of people without many clothes, and the top of every door frame has a triangle cut out so that she doesn't have to remove her hat indoors. However, you don't need to buy expensive crystal balls and curse-nets from ZakZak Stronginthearm, or the craft fair in Slice, to make your house look like a witch's abode. The queue of people at your door will announce it well enough.

Nothing but showy knick-knacks!
- E. Weatherwax

Black Alisss gingerbread cottage

Gingerbread Cottages

This is the type of witch's house you'll have read about in storybooks. But just because you've read about them in fairytales doesn't mean there isn't some truth to it. From what I've been told, there were at least two witches who built themselves gingerbread cottages, Aliss Demurrage, aka Black Aliss, and Granny Whitlow.[1] It didn't end well for either of them. Once you start messing about with fairytales, it's too easy to get caught in the current carrying you towards the story's inevitable end. So, if you absolutely *must* have a gingerbread house, please don't install an oven – especially not one large enough to hold you!

1. *See* Cackling. *Page 172*

Mobile Homes

If you're a witch who likes, or needs, to move around on a regular basis, then a mobile home may be more appropriate. <u>Caravans</u> are particularly handy for witchfinders who travel far and wide to discover young witches, or veterinary witches who may need to spend a few days at a time on a farm. Caravans aren't the only types of mobile home. Nanny Ogg told me that her Genua pen-pal, Mrs Gogol, lives in a hut made of driftwood with a roof of moss. Its mobility is due to its four huge duck feet on which it can apparently scull through the swamps just as easily as it runs through the woods.[2]

I like the fact that a mobile home gives you the freedom to just head up into the hills to be alone for a while. My Granny Aching lived in a simple shepherd's hut on wheels, which she would move to follow her flock. I loved to sit on the front step with her as she wrapped the silence of the downlands around us like a cloak. All she had inside was her narrow bed, a pot-bellied stove, water barrel, food box and lots of stuff relating to sheep. The only decoration being hundreds of blue-and-yellow Jolly Sailor Tobacco wrappers pinned to one wall. Life in a shepherd's hut can be very suitable to practical witches who value the serenity of nature over possessions and decoration.

I'm only sorry I didn't get a caravan sooner. Though I recommend disguising them as a travelling teacher's classroom, or a nomadic fortune-teller's wagon – both of which are slightly more palatable to inhabitants of witch-hostile towns.
– Miss Tick

2. *I only added this because Nanny insisted, however I heard that A LOT of absinthe and something called Banana dak'rys were consumed on that trip, so there's very good reason to doubt the reliability of this story!*

Blind Io,
king of the gods

ON GODS, & OTHER MONSTERS

As a witch you won't just have to navigate the complex world of humans and other witches, but also learn to deal with more otherworldly entities as well. Here's a brief guide to those I've encountered.

Gods

Most witches don't believe in gods. We know that they exist, of course, and we even have dealings with them from time to time, but we don't actually _believe_ in them – we know them too well. Gods are busy* and so are witches, so it's often considered best for both to give each other a wide berth. Rural communities themselves don't tend to have much time for the gods, although I've seen a little flutter of acknowledgement here and there. When Granny Aching died, my father pinned a tuft of raw sheep's wool to the woollen blanket she was buried in. This tradition is to signal to any gods who might be watching that the person was a shepherd and therefore up in the hills all day where there are no temples or churches. Therefore they should definitely take this into consideration and look kindly upon them. I've no doubt that Granny Aching would have had no time for a god that didn't understand that lambing came first.

As witches, the gods you're most likely to come across are not usually the praying-to sort, and more likely the making-things-work sort – like the seasons, nature or the weather. However, don't let that fool you into thinking that having a job will make them in any way more down-to-earth. Although they might have a go at slumming it with the mortals from time to time, they don't tend to be very good at it, and remain as arrogant and infuriating as any other god.

It would be like believing in the postman!

* If that's what you call drinking, gambling and playing around with the lives of mortals.

If you'd like to know more about what we don't believe in then I recommend Chaffinch's Ancient and Classical Mythology.
– Miss Tick

Don't that mention a God of Potatoes?
– E. Weatherwax

Epidity, I believe. And only things Shaped like Potatoes.

Damn! Thought there were finally a god I could get behind! Never met a potato I didn't like.
– Nanny Ogg

I once met Hoki the nature god. Manifests as half-goat, half-man, or sometimes as an oak tree. Bloody nuisance. Terrible flute player too.

That'll be the hooves.

More minor deities tend to be a little more bearable, and I have a particular fondness for Anoia – Goddess of Things That Get Stuck in Drawers. If you happen upon Anoia, make her a cup of tea and don't worry about her chain-smoking of flaming, sparking cigarettes – they're the remnants of her past as a volcano goddess and won't harm the furniture. If she's feeling in a good mood, she will unjam your drawer or unstick your zip. The former is always down to the fish slice. Even if you're sure you didn't own one, that's what'll be causing it.

She's unstuck many a zip for me in a passionate moment.
— Nanny Ogg

The Goddess Anoia Arising From the Cutlery

Gods-with-jobs tend to be very dogged about patterns and routines. The year is round and the wheel must spin. Gods are part of that. If they get thrown off their normal cycle by, say… a silly young witch who inserts herself into the dance of the Dark Morris, and accidentally gets mistaken for the Summer Lady by the Wintersmith, who then thinks he's in love with her and wants to crown her as his queen… well, that can be *very* bad news.

As you've probably guessed, I was that silly young witch, and that was not my finest hour. Keep in mind that sometimes, given the right rhythm, you can find your feet moving much faster than your brain, and then you're in a whole heap of trouble. Before I knew it he was making me roses out of ice and making snowflakes in my image.

I know this sounds all rather romantic, and gods can be good at making you feel that way sometimes. I admit I was a tiny bit flattered at first. But there's a reason love stories between humans and gods never have a happy ending. At least, not for the humans. And for a time my humanity did come into question, because once the Wintersmith saw me as the Summer Lady, for a while, I inherited a little of her powers. Plants grew beneath my feet when I walked barefoot and I was gifted the Horn of Plenty – a cornucopia which spat out food and drink somewhat indiscriminately.

This can happen with other body parts too. Especially when there's a gallon of scumble and a haystack involved.
— Nanny Ogg

I think of this as The Time the kitchen rained Ham Sandwiches.
An' those chickens were damn good layers.
And the beer. It were like having a pub in my front room!

The Wintersmith's misguided courtship

As the Wintersmith continued to woo me, he even tried to make himself into a human by bringing together the elements that comprise a human body from the words of a children's song – *These Are the Things that Make a Man*. Words are important. Even to gods. Yet he didn't understand that the song is not just about what humans are made of, but what humans *are*. No matter how many iron nails or how much potash he collected, he would never be human, and no matter where and who I danced with, I would never be a god. But I could pretend, and I was better at it than him. Remember what I said about gods and patterns? Well, to nudge him back to his old routine of hibernating for the rest of the year, I had to become the Summer Lady and draw down the heat of the sun to melt him and his ice palace, banishing him as she would've done.

When I finally met the real Summer Lady I expected her to be angry – she wasn't. She was <u>entertained</u>. I also thought she'd be all-knowing and wise, but she wasn't particularly smart, or nice, and frankly a bit annoying *and reminded me of a few witches I know*. She was like a regular person who just happened to have a lot of power. Keep that in mind if you ever cross paths with a god. And never accept a reward. There'll be strings attached. They can also be dreadfully smug about rewards. They think that all humans want them. Most of the time they're right, but remember you're a witch and that things being nice and normal and running smoothly is reward enough. Not accepting a reward also unnerves and confuses gods, which is an added bonus.

Gods are like children. They get bored easily. Whilst they ain't particularly forgiving, providing them with entertainment n go a long way.
E. Weatherwax

Nanna name names in those spill words, eh Tiff?
— Nanny Ogg

Lord Lankin, a high-ranking elf

Scunners the lot o' 'em!
— Rob

Elves

I sincerely hope you'll go your whole lives without encountering an elf. They may look beautiful and ethereal, as all the fairy stories might suggest, but really they are nasty, cruel creatures who delight in pain and suffering. They don't understand mercy and are known for their tinkling laughter, which usually means they have managed to corner something weak and helpless. Elves exist in the parasitical world of Fairyland. Having been there, I certainly don't recommend a visit. It's the geographical manifestation of the elves

Tiff ain't exaggerating here. Elves are absolute brutes. Worse than gods!
— Nanny Ogg

themselves. Beautiful, hostile and cruel.

At certain periods, such as Circle Time, when borders between worlds are thin, they like to test the weak spots, looking for a way to breach barriers. They have been successful on more than one occasion, often through human weakness and desire for what they offer, and also when the borders have become weak due to the death of an edge guardian.[1]

If you find yourself in the presence of a creature who seems too beautiful to be true and you feel compelled to please them by whatever means, and yet utterly unworthy of doing so, then you are most probably standing before an elf. There are a few things you need to know in order to have any chance of surviving the encounter.

Be mindful that an elf will only give if they can extract more in return. Like the worlds they come from, they are parasites who play upon our greed and desires. You need to be able to resist this and fight back. This is where iron comes in.[2] It causes them immense pain and can break up any glamour they might be projecting. Without their glamour they appear as tall, thin, foxy-faced humans with greasy hair and an almost tangible animalic stink. Letice Earwig is one witch who seems to be utterly immune to elven glamour, due to an overwhelming amount of self-confidence that has created a kind of mental-iron.

1. *See Edge Witches. Page 40*
2. *See Iron. Page 84*

The glamour is the heart of their power. Break that an' you break their hold.

– E. Weatherwax

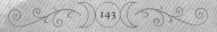

Lady Nightshade,
the queen of
the elves

Elves are attracted to human beauty and creativity. Musicians are a particular favourite. The Feegles admitted to me that when they served the Queen, she'd ordered them to kidnap a few humans to bring back to Fairyland for her amusement. But they took great pains to tell me that they'd never once taken a child. The Queen liked to do that herself.

For the more horticulturally minded witches, be warned that elves are also drawn to beautiful gardens, so beware of exquisite presences drifting through your azaleas. And always know where your trowel is.

Elves are ruled by a <u>king and queen</u>. The queen, unsurprisingly, wields the power. Or at least the king is smart enough to let her think she does. Either way, whoever occupies the position is as ruthless and devious as they come. While an elf queen is only removed by lethal force perpetrated by an ascending new queen, kings tend to come and go with a little more frequency. Sometimes the queen gets bored of them; sometimes she gets really bored of them and the two have Words – the kind of words that level forests and leave deep gashes on the landscape. It has also been known for the king himself to get bored of Fairyland and wander off to a realm that entertains him more.

Whilst I hope I've shared enough to keep you well away from elves, my experiences with the race have not been wholly negative. I have dealt with both an elf king and queen who have been capable of change, of learning and coming to understand humanity

Nae King,
nae Quin,
nae laird,
nae master
we willna be
fooled agin!
– Rob

as more than something to torture. The King who lives under the Long Man in Lancre[3] may exist in the realm of <u>sweaty masculinity and perpetual stag parties</u>, but he was still so intrigued with my gift of his own shed – the one thing no male can ever resist – that he came to my aid during a recent elf incursion.

Meanwhile Lady Nightshade found herself turfed out of Fairyland due to an internal coup, and became something of a … friend. She died protecting that friendship. Died protecting me. If an elf is capable of humanity, then humans have no excuse.

Under the stink and swagger he's not a bad old boy — for an elf.
— Nanny Ogg

Other Creatures of Fairyland

Whilst inhabitants of Fairyland have been beaten back from our world on a number of occasions, elves and their cohorts aren't the type to leave well enough alone. I have no doubt they'll keep prodding at the edges of our world until they find another unwary mortal or <u>unguarded doorway</u> to aid in their return. And since the number of thin places between worlds has never been documented, it's entirely possible that, as a magically inclined person, you might accidentally find yourself in that realm. Or perhaps you might have a small, sticky relative in need of rescuing from it. Whether you meet them coming or going, here are a few notes on some of the other denizens of Fairyland.

This is why you must look to the edges, Tiffany. If I'm not here, it's down to you.
— E. Weatherwax

3. *See* Hill Carvings and Symbols. *Page 99*

Luks like sumfing what fell oot o Big Yan's nose!
— Rob

A typical drome

DROMES

Despite looking like vaguely human-shaped, doughy blobs, the dromes were undoubtably the most dangerous of all the creatures I encountered. They're not native to Fairyland but were snatched from their own world to do the Queen's bidding by weaving dreams to trap the unwary. Dromes raid the memories of the creatures they encounter for the material they need to

Besides us, rite? — Rob

create these dreams from. Human, Feegle or anything else, they'll use whatever they can scavenge.

If you ever find yourself in a dream crafted by a drome, remember never to eat anything otherwise you'll be trapped there forever. You'll slowly wither away to nothing, and the dromes will eat you as soon as you become squishy enough. But, like a spider in its web, you can always find the drome that wove it squatting somewhere in the dream. Once you locate it, it can only be killed by cutting off its head. Imaginary weapons will work for this, although the Feegles tell me that a good kickin' will also help a drome think twice about keeping you prisoner.

Its like tryna kik a tub o jelly
— Rob

One of the biting fey

STINGING FEY

These flying creatures look very much like storybook fairies – tiny, humanoid creatures with either butterfly or dragonfly wings. Storybook fairies are often associated with flowers or other tinkly things like that. However, the biting fey of Fairyland are most definitely not tinkly, unless the tinkle is the sound of something being broken into a thousand pieces. They are exceedingly <u>vicious </u>with mouths full of disconcertingly sharp teeth. View them as flying piranhas.

Dunae go near those lassies! – Rob

The Headless
Horseman

THE HEADLESS HORSEMAN

One of the Queen's most trusted servants, the horseman is often
sent into worlds to assess and deal with dangers before any other
elf ventures through. A susurrus and the sudden onset of snow
can denote his arrival. Despite not having a head, this dark rider
seems to be able to see just fine. The only way that I've found to
unnerve the horseman is to stand your ground and look him in
the eyes. Granted, he doesn't have a head, but you need to look
him in the eyes that he doesn't have.

*There's a lad who's had one
too many scumble hangovers.
— Nanny Ogg*

JENNY GREEN-TEETH

Jenny was the first Fairyland monster I encountered after she turned up in my local stream and tried to snatch Wentworth. When I looked at this water-dwelling monster that had eyes the size of soup plates (I know because I measured them against some of my mother's soup plates) I realized that I didn't feel scared, I felt angry. How dare this ridiculous creature turn up in my land, in my stream and go after my brother! Anger can get you a long way in this world provided that it's channelled in the right way. In my case it was channelled into the clang of a cast-iron frying pan connecting with Jenny's face. That is not to say that feeling scared isn't a natural reaction when encountering otherworldly creatures, but somewhere inside you'll find the anger smouldering. Find it and use it.

A Grade One Prohibitory Monster. One invented by adults to scare children from dangerous places. Please see my book Bestiary of Transient Monsters for more details.
— Miss Tick

Always double check your sources!

Dam it, keep it safe until you need it, then open the floodgates and draw on its power
E. Weatherwax

Jenny Green-Teeth

Three
Grimhounds

*I reckon our Greebo could
take 'em all on!*
— Nanny Ogg

GRIMHOUNDS

These ferocious-looking hounds perform a similar function to
the Headless Horseman, and are often sent ahead to scout other
worlds or protect the boundaries of Fairyland. Visually they are
extremely effective for scaring off potential intruders as they have
flaming eyes and razorblades for teeth. But whilst a headless
horseman can be headless anywhere, glowing eyes and mouthfuls
of sharp metal become detrimental for their owner when
translated into reality. Of course, even then you are still dealing
with a large, angry half-blind dog with blood dripping from its
muzzle, so prepare accordingly.

Bah, ghosties! Ye
cannae giv em a gud
kickin, ye just end up
kickin yer ajn heid!
— Rob

One of the ghosts
of Keepsake Hall

Ghosts

I've encountered a number of ghosts over the years and, contrary
to the stories, most aren't particularly interested in scaring the
living. Many are just stuck in their old patterns or trying to
redress wrongs from their old life, either committed against them
or by them. Keep your wits about you and find out what they
want and whether you can accommodate it.

The first ghost I encountered was Oswald, an ondageist – who,
unlike his supernatural cousin the poltergeist, preferred to tidy
up rather than cause a mess. His history was unknown, but
Miss Level (whose house he haunted) said she always pictured

him as a kind of worried little man with a dustpan and brush.
He certainly could be handy around the house, although he
didn't really get the concept of 'saving something until later' and I
would often find myself fighting with an invisible force who was
determined to tidy away my last half biscuit. Should you ever
find yourself needing to keep such an obsessive ghost out of your
hair for a few hours, Miss Level's advice is to simply mix salt and
sugar together and leave them to reorganize the grains.

Ah, and the
last half's the
best bit!
— Nanny Ogg

   Letitia Keepsake, Baroness of the Chalk and part-time witch,
impressed me with her dedication to dealing with the many
ghosts who haunted her familial home of Keepsake Hall. She
gave a teddy bear to a screaming skeleton to quieten it, and a
pumpkin to a ghost of a woman who had been beheaded and
was perpetually looking for her lost appendage. The pumpkin
had to be changed whenever it got too squashy, but Letitia said
that it gave the ghost comfort, and she suspected it couldn't tell
the difference between a pumpkin and a head anyway.

Might I suggest one
of those pig bladder
footballs which are
growing so popular
in Ankh-Morpork?
— Miss Tick

A hiver, or at least the feeling of one...

Spirits

Whilst ghosts do not usually directly interact with the living (although it can be oddly disconcerting <u>if you accidentally sit on one</u>), you should be aware that spirits are more inclined to seek out a physical body to control. Having been that physical body, when a hiver once took me over, I know all too well what it feels like to have your head crowded with strangers.

I sat on one once. Most peculiar feeling. Had to pop back for a second go.
— Nanny Ogg.

If you are worried about whether someone has been taken over by a spirit, it's important to be aware of who that person was and how they might have changed as their personalities vie for control. Are they busy when they used to be lazy? Quick-witted when they used to be slow? Who are they and what have they become? Under the hiver's influence, I was cruel in ways that still haunt me. Not just for what I did, but for the fact that I could not stop myself from indulging in them. For a moment I lost the anchor in my mind that, until then, I was sure would have pulled me back. Whilst it wasn't exactly evil, the hiver was like many ghosts searching for something, and the key was finding out what it wanted. It turned out that what it wanted was an ending.

However, when it comes to certain spirits, the ending they want is the last thing you should be giving them. They are malevolent and utterly irredeemable. Therefore the ending you must find for them is of the more <u>conventional kind</u>.

While Letitia Keepsake's treatment of ghosts touched my heart, I was a lot less impressed by her accidental summoning of the Cunning Man – a truly demonic spirit of an Omnian witch-hunter who once became obsessed with a young witch. After he lacked the courage to save her from the flames, she saw the true nature of his heart and pulled him into the fire with her, badly disfiguring him. Something snapped inside the witch-hunter and his obsession became a hatred directed at all witches. He deputized more hunters and led a gruesome crusade against the sisterhood. Many women, both young and old, magical or very often otherwise, fell foul of his murderous campaign.

When he died his evil carried onwards, continuing to spread the fear and hatred that drove him in life. But to interact directly with our world, he needs a corporeal body. A <u>human host</u>. Any

A gud kickin? Now yer talkin!
– Rob

Poison goes where poison's welcome.
– E. Weatherwax

The Cunning Man

will do, although he finds a warmer welcome in those who have already embraced the darkness. When the Cunning Man came after me, he took possession of Macintosh, a prisoner from Ankh-Morpork's Tanty prison. The type of person who kills for fun; the ones whose crimes are only spoken of in whispers and all the hangmen are afraid to hang, lest their victim comes back from hell to haunt them.

In his new form, the Cunning Man was able to reignite fear of witches again, even in those who I thought were beyond that. A return to the rough music – the beat of vigilante justice that once sought out any woman deemed too old, too beautiful, too free as the reason for every sick cow, soured milk or missing child. I heard the music coming, and although it didn't claim me, I felt for a moment how thin the line can be between good and evil. Before the Cunning Man's stolen physical body was consumed in a field fire, he reminded me how quickly people can be turned. I smelled the ghostly stink of fear and sulphur. And I knew how close I was to smelling them again. We must remember why we do what we do, we must thicken that line between the smart and the stupid, between respect and disrespect, and hope that the rough music never returns.

Never forget many folks grew up on stories of the 'wicked witch'. She still lives somewhere in the backs of their minds. So you gotta keep telling them a better story. Even if they don't deserve it.
—E. Weatherwax

Especially those who don't deserve it.
— Nanny Ogg

MRS LETICE EARWIG
HIGHER MAGIK, PROFESSIONAL SPELLS

Any aspiring witch should also be aware of the various benefits of evocation of spirits, even demons and deities. Such spirits can be inveigled into assisting in matters such as healing the sick, personal enhancement, to pass on their knowledge of the future, or what we cannot see with our own eyes.

Of course the acts of conjuration and summoning must be carried out with great care. Spirits should never be used for revenge or to settle personal grudges as this would risk the corruption of your soul and provide them with a hold over you. The release or unbinding of spirits, demons and deities is the most important part of the spell for your own personal safety. For well-researched methods and theoretical conclusions, see my upcoming book, *Evoking the Higher Powers*.

PERILS & PITFALLS

I keep sayin'
being popular
ain't important.
Respect is the key.
- E. Weatherwax

Respect is
important, but
people open
up more if they
actually like you
- Nanny Ogg

I don't need to be
liked, Gytha.
Just as well
Esme.

If you are lucky enough to have a steading within a strong and supportive community it can lead you to believe you will be welcomed with open arms wherever you go. However, being a witch can be a dangerous business. We are perceptive, bloody minded and powerful, traits that don't lend themselves to <u>popularity</u>. As well as dealing with external dangers, we must learn to navigate the dangers within ourselves that come with rising power, recklessness and becoming unmoored from our communities and covens. We also deal with magic, and even at the best of times that can be unpredictable and unwieldy, with unforeseen consequences, which is why most of us only use it as a last resort. Here are a few things to watch out for as you navigate the rocky road ahead.

A poisoned apple,
another cackling
classic

Magic

You may think it strange to see magic included in the perils
and pitfalls of our craft, but there are many reasons to use it
very sparingly. Perform too much, too recklessly, and you risk
setting yourself on a path to the bad, or coming to the attention
of beings in search of a powerful host to inhabit. Worse still,
you could attract the attention of otherworldly creatures that
feed on magic. While older witches warn that performing magic
excessively leads you to think you are above all others, witch-
wizard Miss Eskarina Smith told me about other dangers, ones
not of this world. Her words chilled me to the bone. I asked
her to write about them here so that you can learn from her
experience.

The Dungeon Dimensions
by Eskarina Smith

Less than a shadow's width away, in the deep crevices at the edge of Time, lie something wizards call the Dungeon Dimensions. In these desert wastelands, as cold as the night between the stars, live The Things – creatures so horrible that even the dark is afraid of them. They cluster around pockets of magical leakage from other worlds, warming themselves as they probe the walls of reality, searching for a way in.

The Things are drawn to people who not only possess strong magical ability, but who use their magic often. This means that powerful wizards are the largest beacons, as most witches are much less prone to showing off. As the greatest mentor I ever had once told me, 'If you use magic, you should go through the world as a knife goes through water.' While they would cease to exist the second they breached this world, these creatures can successfully invade minds and drag souls into their dimension. I saw it happen to someone I cared for deeply, and I followed him there – to where The Things were waiting.

Magic is useless against these creatures. They feed on it. The most powerful weapon I've found against them is the non-use of magic. Without magic they would die, and when someone with powerful magical ability consciously doesn't use it against them, it causes them something like intense pain and fear. It is the most successful

One of the
cuddlier denizens
of the Dungeon
Dimensions

defence I have found, and the only reason we were able to escape their dimension unharmed. Most are not so lucky and their bodies become vessels for whatever horror finds its way back in their place.

It has been suggested that if The Things ever broke through it would be like an ocean trying to warm itself around a candle – yet still they wait. They are good at waiting.

Mirrors and magic can be a bad combination

Mirrors

Even as an ordinary object, a mirror is a powerful thing. It cannot lie. It only shows us the truth. It can reflect everything, therefore it can also contain it. I've never dabbled much in mirror magic, but Nanny Ogg tells me there's a lot of fun to be had. However, when you start using more than one, that's when their real magic can be unlocked. The powerful can move between mirrors and mirror-like surfaces, and scry through them – which is particularly popular with fairy godmothers, such as the late Lily Weatherwax, and malevolent spirits, including the Cunning Man.[1]

1. *See* Spirits. *Page 155*

There are those who believe that mirrors steal a part of a person's soul. These beliefs are often ridiculed by those who consider themselves above such superstitions. However, just because something is a superstition doesn't mean it's baseless. When you stand between two mirrors and they begin to carry your reflection into infinity the effect can amplify your power. As a consequence, it also stretches you and thins out your soul. Then it's all too easy for a bit to break off and start wandering about by itself. And that just might be the dark part of you, the part you'd rather stayed hidden. Mirrors know and they will seek out the truth. Whilst there is no reason not to keep a mirror around the house – and a small mirror is useful for lighting fires and as a portable scrying tool – be extremely wary of getting between two of them. You never know if the one that walks away will be the real you. Do it for too long and you won't even remember who the real you was.

After I trapped Lily in the mirror, I never wanted one in the house for years. I still catch sight of a reflection once in a while and wonder if it's me or her.

– E. Weatherwax

I once saw her in my best cake knife. Gave me quite a start.

– Nanny Ogg

I still say I would've been better at being bad than her.

Let's not find out, eh?

A bit literal unless a Feegle has just given you a haircut

An Open Mind

They say the trouble with an open mind is that people will insist on coming along and trying to put things in it. For witches the danger of an open mind is quite literal and the things we risk being put in it are downright dangerous. That is to say, spirits of people – the lost, the lonely and sometimes the utterly irredeemable. As you've read in these pages, an early error of mine was to use magic where it wasn't required. Lacking a proper mirror, I stepped outside my body to observe myself, in the way you do when you're borrowing. I knew very little about borrowing[2] at the time and thought it was just a simple parlour trick, but sending my whole mind outside myself left me open and vulnerable.

I was only gone for a few seconds, but when I returned to my mind, I wasn't the only one in there. A hiver had entered, bringing with it a collection of personalities that hummed in the back of my mind like a swarm of bees. I pushed it out once, but it forced its way back in again and squatted there, manipulating my words and deeds, until I found out what it really wanted.[3]

When the hiver possessed me it was like I was a passenger in my own mind – I had been borrowed and was no longer in control. I had to go into hiding within myself until I had the strength to fight back. It left me with an understanding of what it must feel like when a witch tries to dominate an animal's mind rather than travelling as a passenger.

Let this serve as a warning to never use magic on a whim like I did, especially when there are practical solutions to the problem – like finding a bigger mirror! Make sure you never send too much of yourself out there when you use any kind of projection magic, and I recommend casting some form of protection around your body first. Part of you must remain because sometimes the edges we guard are the ones in our own heads.

Both the greatest temptation and peril of borrowing.

– E. Weatherwax

2. *See* Borrowing. *Page 68*
3. *See* Spirits. *Page 155*

The Omnian witch-hunter who was to become the Cunning Man

Witch–hunters

Whilst we've covered the specialism of witchfinding, witch-hunting is something altogether nastier.[4] It's the so-called profession of those who identify, persecute and execute witches. The Omnians, who produced the acolyte who would eventually go on to become the Cunning Man, had a particularly dark history of this. I am assured by current members that this practice has not been carried out by Omnians for over a hundred

4. *See Spirits. Page 155*

years. The priest who told me desperately wanted me to believe him. But it was the kind of desperation where sweat drips out of your ears and you have a <u>look of perpetual panic</u> in your eyes, so who knows if it was really true.

Although we managed to destroy Macintosh, the mortal body possessed by the Cunning Man, we could not destroy the demon inside him. It's out there somewhere, leaking hatred and fear of witches into the world. If you are a wandering kind of a witch, keep a look out for a black-clad figure with a wide-brimmed hat and holes through his head where his eyes should be. This figure will cast no shadow in the sunlight and can often be detected by the rotting stench of his insidious hatred. He smells particularly foul to magic-users, so keep your senses sharp and <u>avoid colds</u>.

Sounds like the look of someone who has recently run into Esme Weatherwax.

— Nanny Ogg

I'm sure I would've been perfectly polite to the good people of the Omnian Church.

— E. Weatherwax

Yeah so polite that a tree would've fallen on them on their way home.

I can't be held responsible for the weather!

The snot goblin is no ones friend.

Try my famous goose-grease-and-sage chest liniment. It keeps all colds away.

True. But that's because the whiff keeps everyone away.

An' therein lies the magic.

THE BONFIRE OF THE WITCHES

Given that poison goes where poison's welcome, witches have tried to stay one step ahead of any would-be witch-hunters. As Miss Tick may have directed you to this book, let me in turn direct you to one of hers, *Magavenatio Obtusis,* which sounds impressive, but loosely translates as *Witch-Hunting for Dumb People.* This contains useful advice such as:

It's very important, having caught your witch, not to harm her in any way (yet!). On no account set fire to her. This is an error beginners often fall into. It just makes them mad and they come back even stronger. As everyone knows, the other way to get rid of a witch is to throw her in a river or pond.

First, imprison her overnight in a moderately warm room and give her as much soup as she asks for. Carrot and lentil might do, but for better results we recommend leek and potato made with a good beef stock. This has been proven to seriously harm her magical powers. Do not give her tomato soup: it will make her very powerful.

It also contains nuggets of wisdom on the correct <u>biscuit</u> to give your witch with her tea in the morning, and what knot to use to tie her up. And most importantly, <u>not to stick</u> around once you've put silver coins in her boots and thrown her in the water. Inhabitants of the many villages where the book turns up don't recall precisely how it <u>got there</u>. But since it's clearly a well-researched and extensive guide, many follow it to the letter. Do your research and if you get a sense that a village you're about to pass through is likely to get match-happy in the presence of a witch, make sure to send a copy ahead!

I recommend memorizing the contents so that, if you happen upon any witch-hunters wielding it, you know what you're up against. As mentioned previously, always keep breathing reeds on you, invest in swimming lessons and keep your knot-untying skills sharp.

They always stick around to watch, which is why we need to be excellent at holding our breath.
— Miss Tick

Biscuits is important. You can tell a lot about a person from the type of biscuit they give a witch. Anything with currants in and you have my permission to curse their oven.
— E. Weatherwax

The Feegles have been very useful in this regard.

And feel free to embrace the drama. Lucy Warbeck told me she flopped about and moaned so convincingly when one of my readers gave her leek and potato soup, that they gave her an entire bucket of crusty rolls, and a few extra pillows.

The 'right sort of biscuits

Cackling

As witches it's our responsibility to keep an eye on one another.
Particularly the less social amongst us. Given what you, as a
witch, might see, hear and do on a daily basis, it's all too easy to
become reclusive and withdraw from the people around you.
And this is where the fairytales have partly got things right.
Because a witch who decides that they've had enough of people,
or starts cackling more than the recommended allowance,[5] is
only a few steps away from moving to a house in the woods made
(improbably) of confectionary items. Then it's only a matter
of time before narrative causality kicks in and suddenly, like
the infamous Black Aliss, you're trying to figure out how many
children you can fit in your oven and measuring up for caramel
beds. Yes, these are as unhygienic as they sound.

Maysherestinpeace.
— E. Weatherwax

It's important to check in with your fellow witches from time
to time. We all have a duty to protect each other from letting the
pressures of the job break us. And if you suspect a fellow witch
of starting to cackle a bit too much, then go for walks, do some
stretches together, make them a nice cup of tea while you subtly
check for gingerbread worktops.

Really, Esme?
After everything
she did?
— Nanny Ogg

I also recommend slipping something a little stronger into their tea. It'll give them
a nice snooze while you cut their nails and give their hair a brush.

5. *Because every witch deserves the occasional cackle from time to time. Just to let*
out the stress.

Weren't her
fault. The stor
caught her. Stor
find a way. They've got a will
live as strong as you or J.

The Stages of Cackling

1. Laughing inside

2. Infectious smile

3. Early-stage cackling

4. CACKLING

PATHS LESS TRAVELLED

By this point, you probably have a fair idea of the ins and outs of witchcraft. At least in theory. Or maybe you're still worried about the craft rules, and where and how they can be bent or even broken. Perhaps you're thinking that there's no place for you amongst us. That you simply don't fit the mould and will never be able to. Before you hang up your pointy hat, let me tell you a few more stories. Some of which are about those who once wondered the same thing, but still found their place by more unconventional means – the part-time witches, the unique witches and those who you wouldn't think of as witches at all. But all with the craft running through their veins, and sometimes a few other things too.

Queen Magrat

Part-time Witches

Being a witch doesn't have to be a full-time occupation. Especially if you've got other things to do, like helping rule a kingdom, starting a family or running a business. Queen Magrat of Lancre and Letitia Chumsfanleigh (Baroness of the Chalk) are two such witches who divide their time between royal duties and more witchly pursuits. Magrat spent many years being a full-time witch and, even though being a queen and a mother takes up a lot of her time, she's still one of the best herbalists around. <u>Even better than Mistress Weatherwax.</u>

As for Letitia, she might look like a watercolour painting of a princess, and she did try

That's because she believes it. Esme knows that coloured water works just as well on some folks. Magrat believes in herbs, Esme believes in people.

— Nanny Ogg

to curse me,[1] but she takes care to visit every new mother on the Chalk, knows how to talk to them, and has even gone into battle against the elves. Her husband, Baron Roland, and I have been friends since I dragged him out of Fairyland, along with Wentworth and an army of Feegles. Aside from a brief period of time when he thought I may have killed his father, Roland has been extremely supportive and respectful of witches. There was a time when things could have been… different with us, but I wouldn't have made a good Baroness. I'm not the best at small talk, I hate the tiny food they serve on huge plates, and I couldn't stomach wearing one of those dresses where you have to walk through doors sideways.

Young Amber Petty doesn't really call herself a witch, but I hope she has a mind to some day. She's the only magically inclined person I know to have officially trained under a kelda, after showing herself to be naturally fluent in the Feegle language, with which even Feegles themselves struggle. She has knowledge of the soothings and a unique bond with animals. She also has a steady husband and is someone who needs a little good in her life – some light for one who has seen so much darkness. She may not choose our path in the end, but it will always be open to her.

They call it 'A la carte' which I think is foreign for 'A la cart it back to the kitchen and get me some proper grub'.
— Nanny Ogg

1. *And instead drew the Cunning Man's attention to me.*

A further note on keldas – I was very grateful for my time as a kelda, but equally grateful to be able to relinquish the role to Jeannie. It's not an enviable task keeping a bunch of boisterous Feegles under control. It's often impossible just to get them all moving in the same direction. It also struck me as a little unfair that, although there is a certain amount of diversity in what male Feegles do within their warrior caste, a female Feegle's path is set from birth. But, even amongst the Feegles there is room to do things differently, or at least the willingness to evolve in that direction.

Part of the reason why Jeannie had so much time to mentor Amber was because her own daughter, Maggie, has shown absolutely no interest in becoming a kelda. Rob Anybody was worried that Jeannie hadn't shared the hiddlins with her, but she had – Maggie was just much keener on joining her brothers in battle. She fought with them against the elves, battling it out as ferociously as any of her brothers-in-arms – perhaps even more so as she felt she had something to prove. Given that the Feegles tend to fight in a chaotic and somewhat haphazard way at the best of times, a warrior with the instincts of a kelda would make a formidable leader on the battlefield.

The lads r jus hi spirited! Jus wait until theys hit sumfin' an' they bounce bak rite nuff!
— Rob

Maggie's a pussle. But she got fite in her worth 12 o the lads. Don tell 'em tho.
— Rob

The Witch-Wizard

When the wizard Drum Billet travelled to the Ramtops to bequeath his staff to the newborn eighth son of an eighth son, he believed that he'd be giving it to someone who would grow up to become a wizard, as is tradition. By some mischievous trick of the gods (who are very into that kind of thing) the son turned out to be a daughter – Eskarina Smith. Initially, it was hoped that she could turn her burgeoning powers towards witch-hood. Mistress Weatherwax took her in as her first mentee and taught her basic herbalism, how to prepare various ointments and infusions, and even <u>borrowing</u>. But it became clear that her magic was more of the wizardly kind and that Esk would suffer by denying that identity.

And so, they both travelled to the Unseen University in Ankh-Morpork where they finally forced change and acceptance within that ancient institution. Of a sort anyway. During her time there, Esk conducted studies into the use of non-magic and learned how to walk through time in what she called the 'travelling now'. The secrets of which she was kind enough to teach me. Eventually Esk decided to return to being a witch on her own terms. She kept her staff, of course. That was hers, no matter what. Although she <u>removed the knob from</u> the end and found it worked much better that way.

She was a natural at first. Then she wanted to control the eagle she'd borrowed. We damn near lost her. She had a bloody wizard mentality back then.
– E. Weatherwax

I hear other wizards wince at the sight of it!
– Nanny Ogg

Eskarina Smith

Mrs Palm

Almost Witches

So honed are the shrewd instincts, entrepreneurship and
protective nature of Rosemary Palm, head of the Seamstresses'
Guild in Ankh-Morpork, that Mistress Weatherwax considered
her to be 'almost a witch'. If you're ever in her part of town,
then Mrs Palm's girls (and a few gentlemen these days) are very
welcoming to witches and will furnish you with a clean room
very cheaply. I recommend turning the red light off though.

Before Esk there had never been a female wizard. But if that's possible then it stands to reason that there could also be male witches. I've certainly met and heard tales of unique men who were blessed with skills that were much more oriented towards witchcraft than wizardry.

Both Queen Magrat and Mistress Weatherwax have spoken highly of Mr Brooks, the former Royal Beekeeper of Lancre Castle. His understanding of bees[2] had an arcane depth to it and he could communicate with swarms as efficiently as their queen. If that hasn't convinced you that there was something decidedly 'witchy' about him, then know that he had formulated a wasp-killer so potent it would actually kill elves.

Another profession that naturally borders on the arcane and unfathomable to most folks is blacksmithing. Obviously with someone like Nanny Ogg as a mother, it would be hard not to get a little dose of witchcraft now and again, but Jason Ogg is a blacksmith of an almost supernatural talent. Years of working with iron have given him the ability to detect the presence of elves, and he also has knowledge of the secret and powerful 'horseman's word', which will calm any unruly horse. As for the art of smithing, there's nothing that Jason Ogg can't shoe. He once shod an <u>ant,</u> and also, at the request of Mistress Weatherwax, put silver horseshoes on a unicorn to break its ties with the elves controlling it.

I recall he stayed up all night with a magnifying glass and a pinhead as an anvil.
— E. Weatherwax

2. And if you haven't worked out from reading this book how important bees are, then you haven't been paying attention.

'Big Red'

And he never hurt it none neither. We used to hear it clattering around under the skirting board. — Nanny Ogg

MRS LETICE EARWIG
HIGHER MAGIK, PROFESSIONAL SPELLS

In this section, Miss Aching alleges that 'Before Esk there had never been a female wizard.' This is quite incorrect as my husband, Doctor Earwig – a retired wizard – will also attest. In fact, the Circumfence island of Krull has been producing female wizards for centuries. The travel writings of the wizard Rincewind even document an encounter with a fifteen-year-old female wizard by the name of Marchesa. The fact that she had already achieved the fifth level of wizardry, and was capable of wielding Ajandurah's Wand of Utter Negativity, leaves me perplexed as to why she was not included in this guide.

Ajandurah's Wand of Utter Negativity

Marchesa
of Krull

Geoffrey Swivel

Just when I thought I had gotten my head around both people and witchcraft, Geoffrey Swivel comes along and shakes everything up. Geoffrey is definitely the person who, in recent years, has not only expanded my horizons, but also made me reconsider some of my ideas about who could and couldn't be a witch. Like many witches, Geoffrey started as someone adrift from his surroundings. Instead of enjoying red meat and blood sports like his father, Geoffrey was a vegetarian pacifist who, along with his extraordinary pet goat, Mephistopheles, spent most of his time reading books.

When Geoffrey came all the way to Lancre to tell me he wanted to be a witch, I asked why he didn't want to be a wizard – the traditional route for a magically inclined young man, which was what I assumed him to be at the time. Geoffrey told me that he didn't think of himself as a man, or anything really. They were merely Geoffrey. And so that's how I've always tried to think of my first apprentice, although there wasn't anything 'merely' about Geoffrey.

I employed Geoffrey initially to help out with chores and preparations. Then we started going round the houses together so that I could teach them some of the fundamentals of witchcraft. I noticed how good Geoffrey was with people, particularly the old men. A calmness seemed to descend on any group, no matter how hostile and riled up, whenever Geoffrey was around. I called it

Geoffrey with their 'nearly new broomstick

'calm weaving'. I don't know if it can be taught and, if so, I hope Geoffrey will consider doing so one day, because it's one of the most impressive skills I've seen. If you want to start yourself along this track, then I recommend becoming an avid observer of people. Not just the things they tell you… or the things they don't – those all important little spill words – but how they exist in the world, how they move through it and how others react to that.

It was through observing some of the locals that Geoffrey saw a need to introduce the old men to sheds. A concept they thought they knew about, but had not yet come to fully embrace. I'll let Geoffrey tell you more about the power of sheds.

The bo-... the la-... the Geoffrey is calm itself. Even after they've gone you feel better about yourself. Like lifes still worth havin.

— Nanny Ogg

ON SHEDS – GEOFFREY SWIVEL

It was when Miss Aching was kind enough to start taking me around the houses in Lancre, that I started to see a quiet sadness amongst the older gentlemen. When once they had been sea captains, businessmen, farmers and soldiers, they now felt in the way in their own homes. While they had been out working, their wives ruled the roost, and they certainly were not going to let their husbands get in the way of the daily running of the household. The wives would cook and clean and busy themselves every second of the day, in an impressive fashion. But, adrift from the working world they once knew, the gentlemen just didn't know what to do with themselves. So, either they risked being cleaned or dusted as part of the furniture if they sat still for too long, or they went to the local public house.

My goat and I tend to do quite well in those kinds of venues and we put food in our stomachs all the way to Lancre through demonstrations of Mephistopheles' counting trick – although it's not a trick, he really can count. I joined some of the locals there and Smack Tremble, Sailor Makepeace and Laughing Boy Sideways unburdened some of their woes to me. They loved their wives dearly, but always felt like they were somehow cluttering up the place or causing extra fuss and worry.

I decided to introduce them to sheds. Not chicken sheds or cow sheds, which they already knew about, but the kind of shed that my Uberwaldian uncle, Heimlich Sheddenhausen, invented – man sheds. A place where they could take themselves off to and customize to their interests. A space of their own for their tools, their fishing gear, their little inventions and projects. Time to tinker in a place to potter.

They started to build their own sheds – each reflecting their personality. Some were immaculate, with every tin and drawer neatly labelled, others were a chaotic mess of scraps and treasures from their old occupations, while there were those that were piled high with half-finished projects. But no matter what their shed looked like, their mood had been lifted. They always had a pot of tea on the go and a full biscuit tin. They whistled again, they hummed, they hugged their wives before they set forth for their kingdom. It might only have been an 8ft by 6ft kingdom, but it was theirs, and that means everything.

The Shed of Doom

Abandon all hope ye who enter!

Of course, some people go rather too far...

I don't pretend to understand the power of sheds in the way that Geoffrey does, but like so many things to do with entities of all kinds, it's about finding out what they want. Even if they don't know themselves. The coming of the sheds created both a gentle community revolution and two important strikes against the elven incursion. Firstly, Mr Sideways invented The Lancre Stick and Bucket Machine in his shed – a giant war-engine that rained down iron swarf on the shrieking elves.

Secondly, I also realized that there was one old boy who might appreciate a shed of his own and got the Feegles to build one for the elf King, by the entrance to his domain under the Lancre Long Man. It was a shed with every fishing fly imaginable, packets of seeds and bulbs, every tool in both stone and wood. Drawers, boxes and tiny tins galore. It intrigued him so much that he came to my aid and dispatched Peaseblossom, the elven leader, and sent the remaining elves hissing and limping back to Fairyland.

I'm not sure if he ever used the shed, but I like to think that crafting a dry fly or placing nuts and bolts in tiny labelled tins might provide him with a delightful distraction from the endless rounds of drinking and debauchery.

So, if you're going round the houses and you happen upon an old gent in his shed, then keep a respectful distance until invited to approach. This is his domain and you need to tread there lightly and infrequently. If he offers you a cup of tea and a biscuit, then you have been accepted into his kingdom.

Damn fine it were. Even had a cludgie. Sumtimes spend time in their meself, when ol' horny aint home.
– Rob

Don't forget the naked wrestling!
– Nanny Ogg

I'm never going to forget that!
– Tiffany

LIFE & DEATH

Wool-brained as sheep might be, J still reckon they learns quicker than most humans.

- E. Weatherwax

In a way, being a witch has a lot in common with being a shepherd. Granny Aching once said to me, 'We are as gods to beasts o' the field. We order the time o' their birth and the time o' their death. Between times, we ha' a duty.' Witches also have a flock and a duty to them. We help them into the world, guard them from threats, treat wounds and illnesses, take away pain where we can. We see the dying safely on their way, then help the bereaved clean them up and lay them out, sometimes offering to stay up to watch over the coffin before the funeral. Then we go home, go to bed and get up ready to do it all again the next day. Witchcraft is about people. Whether or not you like them is of no concern. A witch tends to her flock, no matter what.

Birth

The start and finish of things is always dangerous, lives most of all. Being brought up on a farm, I'd already assisted in dozens of births before becoming a witch. Small hands can be useful when lambing. While the expectant mothers I tended to were all sheep, it gave me a good understanding of what can go wrong and all the things we need to be ready for. You'll learn all aspects of childbirth and midwifery from the witch you are apprenticed to, but if you want to learn from the best, I can recommend staying with Nanny Ogg for a few weeks. She knows as much about delivering babies as she does about all the interesting ways of making them.

And if you'd like an education in that too, better make it a few months! I have songs, stories and informative diagrams.
— Nanny Ogg

There are many things to watch for during births, all of which you'll learn about during your training, but there are also things to look out for afterwards. I once delivered a set of male twins, much to the joy of the family. Then I realized she was having triplets. The last child was a girl and of little importance to the family, who clung to old-fashioned views on the importance of sons. You must watch out for children like this, ensure they don't suffer due to the attitudes of their parents. It's hard, and we can't be there all of the time, but we need to speak up for them that have no voices and educate those who should know better. Don't be afraid to use the power of the hat to lend a little menace to your words if needed.

You means those disgustin' doodles you're always drawing on beermats? You know the village lads trade those with each other for educational purposes?
— E. Weatherwax
And I'm sure the village lasses will thank me for it!

Two copper coins for the ferryman

The Practicalities and Traditions of Death

Taking away pain and easing the passage of the dying is one of the greatest services we can perform, particularly for those who have no family to hold their hand until they pass through the door. The best of deaths are those where we can ease pain and talk away fears and regrets, leaving people with only their fondest memories as they pass.

After the more messy parts of washing and laying out the dead, there are ways of preserving the body if the funeral is likely to take a few days, particularly if loved ones are travelling from afar. If it is possible to place the body on stone, you can use transference of energy to draw every bit of heat from the slab and into a bucket of water. The cold will help keep the body as it has always looked until family arrive.

Be respectful of whatever traditions the family believes in. For example, a dish of earth and a dish of salt are traditional to keep ghosts away. Even if it doesn't actually work, it at least works on the minds of people, and that's what's important. Some will also place two pennies over the eyes of the deceased as payment for the ferryman to carry them across the River of Death.

It is custom for a departing soul to have company the night before a funeral or burial. Often the family watches over them, but when there is no one else, then it becomes our job. Exactly why has never been explained properly, some say we watch to see that no harm comes to them out of the darkness. To make it clear to anything lurking that this person *mattered*. The body may make sounds as it settles down, but you don't have to be afraid of the dead, they don't hurt anybody. It's the living you need to be careful of.

It prevents cases like that old carter over in Slice who woke up and started screaming 'Who turned out the light?' from his coffin in the middle of his funeral. I turned that into one of Shawn and Jason's favourite bedtime stories, until they started waking up screaming whenever I snuffed the lamp!
— Nanny Ogg

The Dark Door

The Dark Door and the Black Desert

We don't often speak of this, but perhaps we should.
Sometimes, at the end of a life, things can go wrong. Someone
may be dying, but can't quite find their way. We need to be there
to help them, to stop them getting lost in the dark. To guide

them to an ending, and perhaps a beginning. There is a door a witch can find if they really need to. Perhaps it's not even a door. Maybe it's a curtain for you, a veil, a portal – whatever makes sense in your mind. For me, it's a dark door. To find it, reach out of yourself. Think about the fact that death is always a hair's breadth away and visualize a portal out of the world of the living. Once you open the door, the soul will know what to do.

    I went through that door once, when I led the hiver to an ending, I can't tell you much about what lies beyond. Only that you'll find yourself taking a journey across a black desert to reach whatever comes next. Whatever that might be is up to you. It was there, on the silver black sand of that desert under the ghosts of long-dead stars, that I first met Death.

An' if for any reason you find yourself guidin' 'em through it, make sure you jam your foot in the bloody thing to stop it closing behind you!
– E. Weatherwax

Death, the Being

People talk of the Grim Reaper as someone to be afraid of. But, despite being a seven-foot-tall, scythe-wielding skeleton in a long hooded robe, with eye sockets that glow blue, he didn't seem like anything to be frightened of. He looks exactly as you'd expect from pictures in books, but I suspect that it's *because* of pictures in books that he looks that way. I saw him again when he came to collect Miss Treason. All I really learned from that encounter was that while you can take the spirit of a ham sandwich through to the afterlife, mustard and pickles tend not to make it.

You'll get to know Death quite well so treat him like any other guest. Offer him a cuppa and a slice of cake. I've heard he also likes a good curry, but I bet it goes straight through him!

— Nanny Ogg

Witches are among the few who <u>can see Death</u>. I've met him many more times over the years, all witches do as we are present for the end of so many lifetimes. People say that he can be vengeful and cruel, but that's not true. He is simply an ending, and a shepherd of sorts. Mistress Weatherwax told me a story once. About a family whose baby boy and best cow had both fallen sick. When Death came for the baby she challenged him to a hand of poker for the boy's life. Death lost the hand and left with the soul of the cow. But Mistress Weatherwax told me that Death had a choice that night. He chose to play his aces as ones and throw the game. So while Death is inevitable – in a very few cases, he is willing to wait.

The Call

At the end of our days, witches have the honour of being collected by Death himself. We are also gifted with the knowledge of when we are going to die, often down to the exact minute. This is referred to as The Call. I don't know how it works, none of us do until we receive it. The information usually comes to us a day or two in advance, which gives us time to clean our cottages, put our affairs in order and pick a successor. Some witches even choose to hold a big going away party instead of a funeral. As Miss Treason pointed out when she sent me out to arrange party food and deliver invitations to her big send-off before she died, 'I don't see why I shouldn't have some fun!'

I won't be sad or afraid when I eventually receive The Call and Death comes for me. Those feelings are for those left behind. I've seen what lies beyond the Dark Door and, as with life, it's just another journey. Many people I've known, and others I've loved, have passed through that door before me. And no matter how long or short a time we have on the Disc, the best we can do is leave behind a life well lived, or at least leave the world just a little better than we found it.

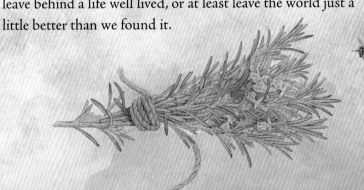

ON JOURNEYS

As I hope the words on these pages have shown you, becoming a witch is a journey. It can take time to find your path, to discover who you truly are, what you want to be and where you belong. Me? I belong to the Chalk. And it belongs to me. As I put the finishing touches to this book, I do so from my very own shepherd's hut up on the downlands, built with my own hands, under the expert tutelage of Mr Block the carpenter, on the iron wheels of Granny Aching's hut. When the business of my days grinds me down, I pull my home to where the larks rise and reflect on who I have become, and the witches and events that moulded me.

Your journey is one that will last a lifetime. It won't be easy, at times the steps will feel heavy and slow, so remember to keep your mind open to wonder. The world is a big and beautiful place. Never close yourself to that. Let it surprise you; let people surprise you. They can and will, even if it takes a little nudging on your part. Never stop learning from the world around you.

I don't wish you luck on your journey – luck is for those who don't trust in themselves. You are witches. Healers of the sick. Midwives and undertakers. Dispensers of Justice. Guardians of the edges and doorways. You are all that you need, but that doesn't mean you should be alone. Love, laugh and live, become part of the community you serve. And while you look to the edges, don't forget to look to yourself. You matter.

From the window of my shepherd's hut I can gaze clear across the downs to the horizon where the sun sets, and watch the moon dance through its guises. As I sit on the step with the breeze on my face and all the smells of nature in the air, I feel Granny Aching and Mistress Weatherwax's hands on my shoulders and know that I can deal with anything. One day you will feel that way too. When that happens, come and find me on the Chalk. Together we will raise a drop of Special Sheep Liniment to all those who guided us – the Weatherwaxes, Oggs, Ticks and Achings of this world. For we are them and they are us.

Tiffany Aching